# Stolen

# Blood

By
R.W.K. Clark

This is a work of fiction. All names, characters, locales, and incidents are
the product of the author's imagination and any resemblance to actual
people, places or events is coincidental or fictionalized.
Published in the United States by Clarkltd.
Po Box 45313 Rio Rancho, NM 87174
info@clarkltd.com

Edition 1

United States Copyright Office
#TX 8-357-780 January 2017
Library of Congress Control Number: 2017907162
International Standard Book Numbers
ISBN-10: 0997876743
ISBN-13: 9780997876741
ASIN: B01MZDMJ7C


/200801

# CONTENTS

# ACKNOWLEDGMENTS

I dedicate this novel to my wonderful readers and for all the amazing people I've met and those I haven't. To my family and loved ones, all your support will not be forgotten.

This book was made possible by reviews from readers like you.

Thank you

R.W.K. Clark

# PROLOGUE

"Loved Ones, Loved Ones. It is time to come to order."

The echo of a gavel rapping twice, sharply, filled the air in the room, and the steady drone of voices, which had been filling it as well, slowly began to taper off. Drinks were set down on the table, and throats were cleared. Within less than a minute the last voice dwindled away completely.

'The Dark Dominant' looked over the scores of people who sat at the massively long rectangular table which spread out before him like an endless highway. All eyes were on him as he stood at his podium, a broad smile on his face revealing his perfect, pure white teeth. His eyes were alight with both pleasure and love for those seated silently and respectfully.

This was the Family of Loved Ones of the Dark Order, children of the Dark Father, better known to the world as Satan. They were those who fed on blood, and for centuries they had murdered for it, but the Dark Father had bestowed a gift upon them which freed them all from very specific aspects of their curse.

Once they were forced to murder, to hide in the day

and come out at night. They had no family, no life outside of their hiding places. But the gift changed all of that; they no longer had to kill to feed, and they were able to live and work among the living, all while enjoying eternal life. They were successes in the modern world, holding high positions and enjoying the luxuries of the world along with all the rest.

My, how things had changed.

His name was Ira Stone, and he was the Dark Dominant, the leader who brought order to the perfect society which, together, all of them had formed. The society was perfect because it existed by the will of their Father, Beelzebub, the one who brought them the success and light they had pursued for centuries... no, millennia. Oh, yes, Stone thought with passion. It was perfect.

Silence now enveloped the candlelit room; not so much as a whisper or murmur came from anyone present.

"Thank you, Loved Ones," Stone continued, his smile still in place as his eyes went from face to face. "This, the monthly gathering of the Dark Order and all who reside therein, has now come to order."

The voices all rang out in unison: "Hear, hear!"

"Tonight, Loved Ones, is a very special night indeed," Stone said as the smile faded from his face. "Tonight we pay tribute to the Father, the one who has given us the prosperity we desired, and the discipline to maintain it without the inner struggle of the ages. But the tribute must be paid in blood that is shed by us; it cannot be bought. It must be taken by force."

"Hear, hear!"

Ira Stone's smile returned, and his icy blue eyes clouded over with perverse pleasure. "I know in what is left of my soul that all of you have been waiting for this night just as I have, for it is tonight that all of us may indulge our true nature once again, though it will be the last time we are able for one full year." He turned to a large wall behind him with a huge black curtain draped over it. The curtain seemed to move in spots all on its own. "I give you 'Brielle'!"

Lights at the base of the wall suddenly came on, illuminating the entire curtain. A voluptuous red-haired woman, wearing only black g-string panties and spiked-heel thigh boots, took a single step forward. She took hold of the curtain and tore it down with a single dramatic jerk. Her smile dripped with anticipation as the curtain fell to the ground, revealing the sight beneath.

A young woman of about twenty-three hung from the wall. Her long, blond hair was drenched with sweat, and her hands and feet were tightly bound, then fastened by the bindings to large iron hoops which were connected to the wall. Her mouth was gagged with a black silk kerchief, and her eyes were wide with terror and tears. The girl was completely naked, and all could see right away that she was flawless, a perfect specimen to be offered to the Father by his Loved Ones.

The redhead turned to those at the table and smiled, her hands and arms spread out before the girl as if she were nothing more than a demonstration on a game show. She then crossed in front of Brielle and struck the same pose on the other side of her. Everyone in the room, including and especially Ira Stone, broke into loud cheers which were saturated with lust and hunger.

Ira Stone turned back to the long table and held up his hands to signify that he wanted quiet, which he got right away. "Now, now, Loved Ones, each and every one of us will have our turn. Once the Father has received the very first portion of Brielle's precious blood, we will each be able to indulge in a single bite. Remember, though, there is no room for greed when it comes to the sacrificial offering. We must share her as though we all were one, and one is precisely what we are."

The redhead suddenly disappeared into the shadows, and the blonde on the wall continued to struggle and sob, but no one paid any attention to her or her emotional state. The way she was reacting was normal; it was something all of them had seen countless times. If she were any calmer, they wouldn't even want her. Her tears were the seasoning on the meal they were about to partake in.

Ira Stone turned his back to the table completely, and faced the girl on the wall, giving her the entirety of his attention. He raised his arms into the air yet again, and after offering the petrified young lady his dazzling smile, Ira closed his eyes and began to speak loudly to the Father of the Loved Ones. His voice was filled with passion and dedication.

"Dark Father," he began, "You have made abundant

provision for all of us, your Loved Ones, your Dark Children. You have allowed us to live and work among those who die, that we may never die. You have ensured that we are fed without others taking notice, yet you indulge our natures with gifts such as the one we have before us, and for this, we are eternally in your debt.

"Some you have allowed to rule corporations; others you have endowed with the knowledge to treat the sick. But there are more, so many more, and you have allowed each and every one of us to be and do whatever our minds desire. We are eternally in your debt."

Stone then reached inside his coat and withdrew a long dagger, the handle of which was hollow, like a tube. He held it high in the air and allowed the candlelight to hit the malicious-looking blade; he even turned it in his hand so the flickering light would dance off the metal. Brielle tried to scream through her gag, but all that came out was a loud, hoarse groan. Her shoulders fell as she lost her strength.

"This is for you, Beloved Father of the Dark Order." Ira Stone, leader of the Dark Order and Chief Executive Officer of Stone & Kimble Pharmaceuticals, stepped forward and drove the knife into the girl's stomach with one fell swoop, his eyes fastened on her face so that he might enjoy the look of pain and terror she gave. Blood began to slowly but surely trickle from the tube which was the knife's handle.

The blood dripped to the floor, where a pentagram was etched deeply in the marble surface. As it dripped, smoke rose from the marble as if Brielle's blood were actually burning it. A sound like distant screams of joy filled the air; it was not coming from anyone present in the room, though. It was coming from the Dark Father himself, and his minions.

The room stayed quiet for exactly six minutes. Brielle's blood trickled slowly, oh, so slowly, during that time. When exactly six minutes had passed, Ira Stone withdrew the knife from her flesh, turned to the others at the endless table, and held his arms up for a final time.

"Dine!" he screamed, his eyes flashing. "Partake of the Dark Father's blessings and eat your fill, each one of you, one at a time!"

All of those around the table rose slowly, men and women alike. They formed a long line, which seemed to fill the entire room. Each of them mumbled prayers of thanks as they waited their turn to take a single bite from anywhere on the girl's body, which was still twitching with life when the first few bites were taken.

From someplace unseen, a trombone began to play…

# CHAPTER 1

"Raina, how many nurses do you have scheduled for the day?"

Vincent Brodsky stood at the main desk of BioDonor, a chain blood donation company with this particular site located in Philadelphia. He was flipping through a stack of papers which were fastened securely down to a clipboard, trying to figure out how many he would have on staff for this busy Monday morning. Raina Gall was straightening magazines and chairs in the waiting room, bending over each and every table as she did so. Vincent stared at her with great lust; he had considered many times what it would be like to have her, but he had always held back. The director, Melvin James, often spoke of never mixing work and play, and Brodsky couldn't lose his job, at least not yet. Maybe after another few illegal blood sales, he could begin to consider it.

"I have seven scheduled, Mr. Brodsky," she replied as she paused to consider his question. "I hope that's enough. I guess it does depend on how many drop-ins we actually get, though."

Brodsky tossed the clipboard down on the hard

countertop in frustration, causing it to clatter noisily on the surface. He shook his head in disgust. How could he ever consider banging such an incompetent pain in the neck? Having a great rear didn't make up for lack of dependability. Exactly how many times had he told Raina to schedule two more nurses than what they would need for scheduled donations, especially on a Monday? At the beginning of the week, and mostly toward the end of the month when people were really broke, they proved to need more nurses than they always anticipated to conduct the blood and plasma draws. Vincent Brodsky stood there and allowed himself to indulge in visualizing himself strangling his head RN rather than ravishing her.

After a moment of self-indulgence, the manager of BioDonor glanced at his antique wristwatch: six forty-five. "Well," he said to her sternly, offering her a cross look as well, "I see we have a full day as far as actual donation appointments go. Who knows how many drop-ins will decide to pay us a visit. I suggest you try to get a couple more nurses to come in, or you are going to be putting in at least three hours of overtime this evening. How's that for a fabulous Monday, Ms. Gall?"

Brodsky turned on his heel and headed back toward his office with steps that were both pissed off and determined. Raina Gall stuck her tongue out at his back and headed for the desk. He was right, and she knew better than to understaff on a Monday, but she had to pull teeth just to get the nurses that were on the schedule to agree to come in at all. They simply didn't make enough money working at a donation center, and many of them were seeking out more lucrative employment during the days they did have off.

Back in his office, Vincent Brodsky plopped down at his desk and began to rub his temples. How he hated stress, but it seemed that was all he had as of late, especially since he had been running a number with the mayor of Philly, Mason Stout himself. Stout was also running for governor, and it seemed that since the race had begun the man had upped his demands for product, doubling them. Brodsky needed as many nurses in there as he could bring in, because he needed all the extra blood donations he could get.

It wouldn't do to steal blood donated at legitimate appointments. That blood and plasma was carefully documented. But the drop-ins and their donations were another story entirely. Vincent had special 'paperwork' that was filled out for them, and the gist of it was that the special paperwork was nothing but smoke and mirrors. He paid them thirty dollars per donation, just as he did the rest, but that money came out of his pocket, and their blood made a beeline for the back door and Mayor Stout.

What did a man like Mason Stout want with a bunch of blood, anyway? Well, Vincent had asked himself this on numerous occasions, but the money was so good that he simply pushed his questions out of his mind. Besides, it wasn't like he dealt with Stout directly. No way, Jose. There was a 'middleman' who took care of all the business. He was a business acquaintance of

Vincent's, sure, but Stout had the man firmly in his pocket. Brodsky asked no questions, and no one told any lies.

Except for Brodsky, to his staff, of course.

A sharp knock came at his office door.

"Mr. Brodsky?" It was Raina.

Vincent shook his head rapidly, as if to clear it, then picked up a pen so he would look busy. "Yes?"

Raina entered the office a bit timidly. "I have Smith and Caine coming in to help today."

"Good, good," Vincent replied. "Put them exclusively on walk-ins along with Thompson. I'll go ahead and help with walk-in paperwork so you can focus on appointments, got it?"

"Yes sir."

Raina left the office, and Vincent let out a huge sigh of relief. He felt immediately better as if a huge weight had been taken from him. Ross Berry, Mayor Stout's middleman, was going to be there Thursday evening to make a purchase, and Brodsky was significantly short on the order as of this morning. Now he would be able to make the quota, and Stout would be satisfied.

Eight gallons of blood, Vincent thought to himself. What could someone possibly want with eight gallons of blood per week? He could only assume that the man was somehow involved in the medical black market. Vincent knew that other countries, which were less fortunate, would need blood, not to mention underground abortionists and scientists who were conducting unapproved testing. Yes, it was more than likely something like that; what else could it be?

He picked up his phone and quickly punched in a number. It rang numerous times before going to voicemail, so he hung up and then redialed. This time it was answered on the first ring.

"Berry."

Vincent cleared his voice. "Berry, this is Brodsky. I'll have the order ready and waiting for you at seven Thursday. This time, make sure you have all the funds. It's getting too difficult to meet the orders, and I need to be able to count on you to pay the right price. Agreed?"

"Yeah, I'll have it. See you Thursday."

The phone went dead in Vincent's hands, so he hung up without another thought. A quick glance at his watch told him he needed to get out there and start getting ready for the drop-ins. BioDonor opened at eight, and drop-ins usually started coming almost immediately. He stood, put on a white jacket, and headed out of his office.

It would be a busy day.

∞

Ross Berry hung up the phone without a second thought and headed into his bathroom for a shower. It was Thursday morning, and he just reverified the blood pickup with that chump Brodsky from BioDonor. He needed to call his friend and partner, Mike Biela, but the lazy prick wouldn't be up yet. He would shower and eat, then call the bum and tell him they would leave for Philly around two in the afternoon.

After he finished with his shower, he toasted a bagel and ate it dry while standing at the sink. Ross chewed slowly and stared straight ahead, wishing he had some cream cheese or jelly, or anything to moisten up the dense bread, for that matter, but he was broke. At least he was until that evening. Then he would pick up some groceries.

He swallowed his last bite and chased it with a cold cup of coffee. He was still thinking about money. No, it was true, he shouldn't be broke. After all, he had just made two grand last week from his last pickup for Mayor Stout, but the horses had a way of calling his name; he had managed to break his bank within less than two days. Yep, he thought, I need to get groceries before I even think about hitting the track.

Ross thought briefly about giving up the gambling for the millionth time. Maybe he should find a nice girl, get a house, and have two-and-a-half kids or something. The thought made him smile, but only for a moment. It was an unlikely thought. What would he do while he was looking for this dream girl, anyway? No, he wasn't giving up playing the horses any time soon, and he knew it.

Next, Ross dialed Mike Biela's number on his cell phone. Time to get the lazy bum out of bed. It was going on ten now, and he wanted to have Mike in the van by a quarter of two. If he waited, the guy wouldn't be ready on time, even if he did have just under three hours to get ready. Being a slacker was a pattern for Mike.

It wasn't like Ross needed him for anything. On the contrary, the only reason he brought Mike and tossed a grand at him every week was because of the danger of dabbling around with the black market on a solo basis. It was safer, and smarter, to do business in pairs or more. It was a lesson he had learned the hard way five years prior when trying to move some diamonds for some South African dude; he wound up losing a pinky finger to the man, who tortured him for hours trying to get the name of his fence. No, Ross Berry wouldn't make that mistake again, even if it did cost him a thousand dollars a week.

Mike's phone rang once, twice, three times. He answered, his voice groggy and thick with sleep.

"'Ello? Who's there?"

Ross smiled slightly with amusement at the sound of his friend's voice. "It's time to get moving. Time to get your butt out of bed."

"Ross?" Mike grunted a bit, and Ross could imagine him trying to sit up. He heard a lighter lighting and knew that Mike was firing up a cigarette. "What time is it?"

"Nearly ten," Ross replied.

Mike inhaled deeply. "Ten? What the heck, man? Why so early?"

"Early? Most people have been at work two or more hours by now, you damn vagrant." Ross shook his head in disgust. "We have our run today; it's a go-ahead. I need you ready by one-thirty, and I want to be on the road to Philly by a quarter of two."

Mike broke out in a coughing fit, and Ross waited patiently. After choking for what seemed like an eternity, Mike said, "You could've let me sleep another hour or two; we have plenty of time, man."

"No, Mike. You don't have plenty of time," Ross said with disgust. "I doubt very highly that you got laid last night, and it will take you an hour just to get up from the bed to take a piss. Stay up, because I'm going to be there, and you better be ready, or I swear, I'll keep your money, man. Just be ready."

"Yeah, yeah," Mike retorted impatiently.

With that, Ross hung up. He wasn't going to prolong an already-painful conversation. Mike would be ready, he knew that, but it would be only because Ross rousted him out of bed four hours ahead of time.

Now it was time to go clean out the van. He hated a messy vehicle, and Mike always managed to litter the passenger side substantially. Ross only used the white panel van for these runs, so he hadn't cleaned it out from last week. He drove an old rusty sedan during the week, and out of sight was out of mind.

Cleaning out the van was a quick and easy task: empty the ashtray, throw away the fast food cups and wrappers from the passenger side, and drive it to the car wash, where it would undergo a speedy vacuum and drive-through wash. Within a half-hour, Ross was parked back at his trailer with a little camouflage Christmas tree hanging from his rear-view mirror that reeked of cedar wood.

Now to wait. Ross locked himself into his trailer,

where he took a blue spiral notebook from his desk. He began to do some simple math in the back, then afterward he flipped to the front. Now he used his smartphone to check out the horses and their numbers, and he made his decisions, recording them in his notebook.

Soon he was punching numbers into his phone and placing bets. When you have nothing to do but wait, why not pick your ponies and place your bets? He thought. Ross Berry chuckled at this personal joke and waited for his bookie to answer the line.

# CHAPTER 2

Mayor Mason Stout strode confidently off the elevator and across the reception area floor outside of his office. He offered a sexy, alluring smile to his assistant, Lucy Kayman, who gave him a very naughty one in return. The sun shined brightly in the window and warmed Stout's face as he paused before Lucy's desk. Oh, how he loved being able to enjoy the sunlight so; the feeling simply never got old.

"Good morning, Lucy." His voice was deep, and he purred like a cat staring at a waiting meal. "We have a very busy day, now, don't we? Messages and daily agenda, please, dear?"

Lucy gracefully flipped open the cover of a black leather day planner and ran a blood-red tapered nail across the top of the page.

"At nine thirty, you have your initial press conference regarding your run in the gubernatorial race with Channel Thirteen news," she began. "At eleven-thirty is your luncheon with Gabriel Stark. When you return you have a two o'clock with your staff here to discuss the Kristie fundraiser next weekend, and at four you have an interview with Philadelphia Today magazine." She paused. "Oh, yes, and you have your weekly meeting with Mr. Berry tonight at seven."

Mason nodded at her. "Perfect. Any calls?"

"As a matter of fact, Ira Stone called about fifteen minutes ago. He asked if you would call him as soon as you got in." Lucy gently closed the book, and a smile curved slyly over her lips as she peered up at him. "Perhaps if you find you have any... spare time in your schedule, you could consider fitting me in? I keep late nights, you know, 'Misssster' Stout."

He chuckled and flicked his tongue luridly over his lips. "I know that you do, Lucy."

With no further ado, Stout continued on into his office, neither validating his assistant's innuendo or telling her goodbye. Her eyes followed him as he walked away and secured his office door behind him. Then she rolled them and turned back to her computer. Mason was forever the flirt, but she had yet to sample his wares.

In his office, Mason removed his suit jacket and hung it from the tree next to the door. He then took his attaché case and took a seat behind his desk, setting the bag neatly on the floor beside him. First things first: call Ira Stone. It simply wouldn't do to leave the man waiting for any longer than he had to.

Stout dialed the telephone with such speed and grace that the movement of his fingers could not even be detected by the naked eye. He was unaware of it, though. The way he moved, spoke and even looked was attributed to the nature which he had acquired, the nature which he had been given. He closed his eyes and leaned his head back against his tall-backed chair, letting the sun from the window stream in on his face.

"Ira Stone."

Mason smiled. "Hello, Ira. I hope this beautiful day finds you energetic and well."

"Mason!" Ira exclaimed. Though his voice was low, the pleasure in it was unmistakable. "Indeed, it does. Thank you for returning my call so expeditiously. I hope you have good news for me."

Mason's eyes opened, and he leaned forward, placing his elbows on the blotter on his desk. "Of course. Everything is a go, as it always is. I will meet Berry this evening as usual. Why are you concerned?"

"Well," Stone said slowly. "You mentioned during our last call that the connection for your sector was rumored to be… short on supply this week. I take it that is no longer the case?"

"My man hasn't contacted me to confirm that," Mason replied. "I am confident that no news is good news, Ira. Besides, no matter what my supplier's state is, I will provide for those in need under my care. I would never put any of the Loved Ones in a predicament where they might be forced to compromise the blessed position which we are all in."

Ira Stone breathed an audible sigh. "Good. I would hate to think that, after all the Dark Father has blessed us with, we would have to jeopardize our newfound peace and lifestyles by turning back to the old ways. No one in the Family can afford that, you know. We are all living life at the pinnacle."

Mason Stout remained silent for only a moment, until he was sure that Ira was done speaking; he was the Dark Father's High Priest, after all. "I keep close tabs on all the Loved Ones in my sector, Ira. I would never tempt them to displease the Father by putting them in a position of hunger or lack. I would take care of the problem immediately, if there was one to take care of. But fortunately, all is as smooth as... silk, shall we say."

"Good, good," Ira concluded. "I will speak to you this evening then, as I will to all the other sector leaders. Say, around eight thirty?"

Mason smiled again, but this time because his patience was wearing thin. "Likely sooner, Ira Stone."

No more words were said because there were no more to say. Both of them hung up at the same time, and with that, the conversation was over. Mason steepled his fingers beneath his chin and rested his head there.

Next on the agenda was his nine thirty press conference for the governor's race. He felt totally at ease about the appointment. After all, the Dark Father had ordained this. He would walk in this position for as long as he was destined. If the rest of the world had any idea how many Loved Ones were roaming the Earth, they would see reality for what it really was.

Vampires ruled everything. They had all the power, and it was given to them freely. Fortunately for these disgusting mortals, none of them hunted anymore. No, the blood they required was provided to them generously and graciously.

Mason Stout had a bit of time before his conference. Perhaps he would go seduce Lucy Kayman for a while. That should pass the time quickly. He did have an insatiable appetite for all things sexual; that hadn't changed at all when the Dark Father bestowed the gift. Sometimes it was so overpowering that Stout would go through three women in a single night. It wasn't hard since he wasn't burdened down with a wife.

At first, he had been concerned that the fact he was unmarried would hinder his chances for office. But Ira Stone and his assistant, Thorne Braun, had taken his concern to the Father and they had been told to put it out of their minds. Surprisingly, no one even brought up the fact that he wasn't married and had no children. The public seemed to embrace a fresh face that wasn't distracted by a woman and family. The Father had made it so, and he did it immediately.

Now, all Mason had to do was be sure to live under the protection of the gift, and all would turn out exactly as planned.

∞

The resistance and negative emotion which Ira Stone felt from Mason Stout through the telephone was tangible. The man envied Ira's high position. He wasn't satisfied to be in a lucrative spot himself. Mason Stout believed in his black heart that he deserved even better; he should be a priest to the Dark Father. While Mason was Family, he lacked one thing: the ability to let go of his selfishness, even if it meant handing it to the Father.

It could turn out to be a problem for the entire Family, but for now Ira Stone was going to have to deal with it the way a Dark Dominant was expected to.

But it was as it was. Ira had been handpicked from all of the Loved Ones to hold the position he held, and not Mason or anyone else had any business questioning it. Truthfully, Ira was surprised that the Father had not yet wiped out Stout for his arrogance, but that was none of his business either. He must tread lightly, so as not to be the one to cast a stone when he was just as vulnerable to the Father as anyone.

But along with his position came much responsibility, and that included ensuring that the Loved Ones all received the nourishment that their breed required to survive. If they did not, it would be only natural for them to hunt in order to eat, and the Father had forbidden it; he had a much more extensive agenda in mind, and to bring it to fruition required strict obedience. So Ira would do his job flawlessly if it was the last thing he did.

He had a long list of sector leaders he had to touch base with each and every week, and they were all over the world. Ira glanced down at the parchment on his desk with his flowing script on it. Next on the list of calls to make that day was none other than Gabriel Stark. Stark was the president of the largest and most lucrative engineering firm in the world, Stark Engineers USA. Ira had very little doubt that Stark had all of his ducks in a row. He was somewhat obsessive when it came to pleasing the Dark Father, and Ira knew he was one of the last to worry about, but the call had to be made anyway.

As he dialed, he considered the fact that Mason Stout had a luncheon scheduled with Stark for that very day. He also wondered if Stout, in all of his sex-obsessed glory, had any idea that Ira knew every move he, and everyone else made, at all times. He was sure Stout did; it would be foolish to think that the Dark Father didn't keep his right hand up to speed on what the left hand was doing.

The phone was ringing, so Ira Stone cleared his head and set his focus. He hoped that Mason Stout would come around and stop being so flippant when it came to the needs and desires of the Loved Ones as a Family. But until that day, Ira would do things the way the Father directed him to do them.

# CHAPTER 3

At a quarter of twelve, Ross Berry decided to step out and get a bite to eat for lunch. He had only two hours until he had to pick up Mike Biela for the trip to Philly, and he thought if he had to put up with another second of Jerry Springer reruns, he would hang himself. So, he eagerly grabbed a jacket, shut off the television, and nearly tripped over his own feet running out the door.

As he sat in the drive-through at Super Burger, Ross realized he had forgotten one important thing: he hadn't called Mason Stout to confirm that the order would be ready. That should have been the first thing he did after speaking with Vincent Brodsky from BioDonor that morning. His stomach sank; Stout was surely pissed, even as he sat there waiting for his Super Bacon and curly fries, and Ross knew it. There was only one thing he could do: pull over when he got his order and call the man up right away. He was in for a good chewing-out, but there was no avoiding it. It was the best choice. The only alternative was to ignore making the call and quite possibly get the crap kicked out of him by one of those spooky heavies who were always tagging along with the mayor.

Ross paid for his order and snatched the bag of food from the attendant's hand, then quickly pulled out and into the closest parking space. Tossing the bag on the passenger seat of the van with one hand, he began to dial Mason Stout's personal number with the other. He didn't even bother to put the van in park; he just held his foot on the brake to keep it in place.

"Do you have any idea how much I despise undependability?" Mason immediately stated upon answering. "I laid my expectations out to you clearly and concisely from the very beginning, yet you persist in being irresponsible and making me worry. I have others in charge that I must deal with!"

Ross took a deep breath. "Yes, Mr. Stout, I do, and I can't apologize enough. Everything is a go, and I will see you at seven."

"Yes, you will, and then we will go over your inability to be responsible," Stout said in a deep, irritated voice. "Shit rolls downhill, you know. And a fair share hit me this morning. I hold you responsible."

He hung up the phone and Ross just stared at his cell, his hand trembling. Well, there was nothing he could do now but get the job done, and make sure to straighten up in the future. Stout had an impeccable reputation as mayor, and he would maintain it during the governor's race. But Ross had a strong feeling that he could deal with his problems cleanly and quietly, and never get any of the mess on himself.

Maybe he really did need to give up the horses, if

only for a while.

He looked over at his Super Burger bag and rolled his eyes; suddenly his appetite was completely gone. He had to eat, though, or his blood sugar would drop. He would force himself in a bit.

Well, there was really only one thing to do, he thought as he glanced at the clock on the dashboard: head over to pick up Mike a little bit early. They would hit the road for Philly and reach their destination ahead of time. He knew he wouldn't be able to close the deal with Vince Brodsky until the usual time, but taking off now would keep him from obsessing over his unsettling conversation with Mason Stout. The guy creeped him out, and he always had.

There was something different about the Philadelphia mayor, something... spooky, but Ross never could put his finger on it. His voice never raised above a certain level, even if the situation called for anger or outrage; it could be detected clearly just by his tone, and that was frightening. Also, he always had this disturbing smile on his face, sort of like the cat that just ate the canary, or someone who knew a big secret and was holding it back for future ammunition. The most unsettling thing of all had to do with the blood. When Ross would make delivery of the goods to Stout, he would always give the shipment a good once-over. That wasn't what was weird; it was normal business practice. But he would sort of flick his tongue over his lips as if he were licking them, and he did it only at the sight of the blood. What kind of weird habit was that, anyway?

Yeah, Ross thought. He's a strange one, all right.

He took a deep breath and fished his burger out of the bag. After unwrapping it, he started the van, put it into gear, and backed out of the parking space. Taking a big bite out of the sandwich, which he could barely chew because his throat seemed closed up, he put the van into drive and squealed out of the Super Burger parking lot. He cleared his mind and set his focus on getting to Mike's house, and he allowed himself to think about nothing else.

Time to get the show on the road.

∞

Mike Biela looked at the clock on his outdated flip phone: one fifteen.

He tossed the butt of his smoking cigarette on the ground and stamped it out with his foot. Ross wasn't supposed to pick Mike up for another half-hour, and when he called to let him know he was on his way early, Mike was still in his boxers. Pissed, he stood up and began racing around his pitted-out, one-room apartment trying to get ready fast. Now he'd been standing outside waiting for Ross to arrive for ten minutes. He could've sat on his bum a little longer, which just happened to be his favorite thing to do in the whole world.

Mike and Ross had been friends for years, since junior high school. They had always been involved in some kind of crime or other shenanigans for years. If they weren't selling drugs, they were robbing houses or running bad checks. Ross had a gambling habit to feed, and Mike had been a pretty severe addict in the past.

Now, he was just lazy and greedy. The money he made from this little 'job' made it all worthwhile, and that was a fact.

He didn't have to accompany Ross on these little deals, but Ross didn't like to do business by himself. He never said why, but Mike was pretty sure it had something to do with Mayor Stout. Yeah, he was a bit of an odd duck, but Mike didn't see any reason why Ross should be put off enough by the man to part with a full grand a week. Well, whatever floated his friend's boat. He wasn't about to look a gift horse in the mouth. He'd put up with shifting schedules and pushy partners all day long for a free thousand every seven days. It kept him from having to suffer the nine-to-five grind like all the other idiots.

Just then, Ross Berry's white-panel van pulled into the parking lot of the slummy apartment building. Mike grunted and smiled as he stepped away from the building and waited for Ross to bring the van to a full stop. The man just stared straight ahead and waited for his friend to get into the van.

"Hey, bud," Mike greeted him as he pulled himself into the passenger seat and slammed the door. "Why the sudden change of plans, man?"

Ross put the van in gear so they could get going. "It was my own fault. I forgot to call Stout after I talked to Brodsky to tell him everything was a go. He was a bit pissed, though you wouldn't know it just from his voice. Anyway, you know me and my nerves. I couldn't just sit and wait for time to pass when the customer is on edge, you know?"

"Yeah, yeah," Mike replied with a wave of his hand. "You need something, man. I swear you are gonna put yourself in an early grave. Want me to run into Kimmie's for a little stash to calm your nerves?"

Ross ignored the question and turned on the radio to stop the conversation and pulled the van into traffic. Within twenty minutes they were merging onto Interstate 476, leaving the town of Emmaus, and their shabby homes, behind them. For Ross, it was always good to get away from town, but the track near Bethlehem was always his favorite escape.

They rode in silence for the first half-hour, oldies pumping out of the radio speakers and the windows cracked to let the cigarette smoke out. It took only around an hour and a half to get to Philly, but Ross had to stop and get the coolers to put the blood in when they picked it up, and the paperwork to rent the darn things always took forever to fill out. Then they would eat something before meeting up with Vince Brodsky in the alley behind BioDonor. The whole thing was a process, but it was well worth it for the three grand total it brought in.

The last two-thirds of the drive consisted of Mike chain-smoking while telling Ross unlikely tales of all the girls he laid in high school. Ross listened half-heartedly, emitted the occasional obligatory chuckle or 'heck yeah,' and let him rant. By the time they reached their exit in Philly, Ross not only wanted to strangle his trusty friend and passenger, but he also wanted to dump his body at some secluded rest area as well.

It turned out to be a good thing that they left Emmaus a bit early, however. The first rental place, the one they always went to for the refrigeration units, ended up being one unit short. Some idiot had rented one and never brought it back, and they couldn't seem to get a hold of the guy for a return. Ross went ahead and rented the three units they had on hand; then, he had to sit in the van on his cell phone calling other rental places until he was able to track down one more available refrigeration unit. The drive across town and the additional time he had to put in for paperwork cost them another forty-five minutes; it was nearly five o'clock by the time he had the units up and running in the back of the van so he could be sure they were cool enough to keep the blood.

"All right," Ross said as he finally climbed into the driver's seat. "Looks like we're gonna be all right after all. I was a bit worried there."

Mike rolled his eyes, but he had to admit, he had begun to worry as well. The last thing he needed was to have come all this way only to not get paid. "So, where do you wanna eat?" he asked Ross.

Ross was pulling back into traffic and didn't want to take his eyes off the road. "What time is it again?"

"Just now five," Mike replied.

Ross grunted and chuckled a bit. "Whew. We are in good shape. Instead of stupid Super Burger let's go in a sit-down somewhere. You know, a real restaurant." He began to scan the businesses along the avenue in search of ideas.

"There's a place," Mike said as he squinted at a building to the right. "Leo's Diner." He turned to Ross. "Wanna eat at Leo's Diner?"

Without answering, Ross hung a quick right into the crowded parking area of the small café. He parked quickly and turned to his sidekick. "We'd better hope they don't have a waiting list; the lot's pretty packed. And you'd better hope they have Reubens because I have been wanting a Reuben really bad."

The two men got lucky on both counts: no wait, and Reubens to spare. Soon they were sitting in silence at a tiny Formica table for two, shoveling sandwiches and fries into their faces and chasing the food with bottles of beer. Ross glanced at the clock on his cell phone often, but overall he was pretty relaxed.

He would save his tension for the meeting with Mason Stout, and it was just around the corner. For now, he was going to do exactly what his sidekick was doing: relaxing and enjoying his food and drink. He made Mason Stout and the meeting the furthest things from his mind as quickly as he could.

# CHAPTER 4

"Guys, hurry up!"

Vincent Brodsky stood at a small window next to the back entrance at BioDonor, watching for Ross Berry and his squirrely friend to arrive. He was the only one in the building, so he shouldn't be nervous, but he went through the same emotional roller coaster every Thursday evening. All it would take for his career to end was for just one of his employees to forget a purse, jacket, or some other worthless item. They would return in hopes he would still be there, and then the jig would be up. Vincent had no business being there this far after hours, and everyone knew it. If anyone ever showed up, they were either up to no good, or they were onto him and trying to bust him. Either way, it was far more than he wanted to ever have to deal with.

Oh, he took an abundance of precautions. His car was parked up the block and around the corner, for one. Secondly, he made sure all the lights were out, and doors were locked. But there were still a couple of nurses, one being the head nurse Raina Gall, who had keys to the building, the other being Melvin James, the director. When he waited here like this, it felt like the adrenaline running through his veins was on overload. He practically vibrated.

Suddenly, to the right of the building, he saw the headlights coming around to the back of the building. Vince held his breath without even realizing it, as he waited for the vehicle to come into sight. When he saw that it was indeed the same white van as usual, he let out a breath of relief that could've blown back someone's hair.

He reached down and flipped the large deadbolt, then cracked the door and waited for Ross to shut off the ignition to the vehicle. Soon the two men were getting out of the van and walking silently toward the door. Vince held it open and stood aside, making way for them to enter the building unhindered.

Once the door was shut and locked Ross said, "Evening, Vince. Hope the week has treated you right."

"Right as rain," he replied, as he began walking down the hall to refrigerated storage with both men on his heels. Vincent Brodsky wasn't really one for small talk, especially when it came to the weekly deal he was involved in. The last thing he wanted or needed was to make friends out of either Ross Berry or his companion, so he always kept conversation minimal, and never discussed his personal life.

The men entered the walk-in refrigerator where Brodsky had stacks of small Styrofoam coolers waiting just inside the door. Ross gave them a quick count and, satisfied with the number there, reached inside of his jacket and pulled out a yellow, sealed envelope. He handed it to Brodsky and gave a nod to Mike, indicating he should start loading the van with the containers.

"You'll find it all to be there, just like usual," Ross said.

Brodsky broke the seal, glanced inside the envelope, and then tucked it inside of his own jacket. "Thanks, guys. Guess I'll see you next week. Try to load these up fast; you know how paranoid I am."

Ross grabbed two coolers. "Got it; we'll be out of your hair in just a bit."

It didn't even take ten minutes for Ross and Mike to transfer the goods to the van, and soon they were on the road. Now the next step was to head for Mayor Stout's mansion, where they would pull in the rear and park the van inside a loading garage. Stout had men that would unload the van for them, and then they would get their weekly fee of three grand. Before they knew it, they would be heading back to Emmaus and their shabby little homes, but of course, once Mike was dropped off Ross would be getting in touch with his bookie and focusing on the big races.

Once they were inside the garage at Stout's place, Ross jumped out of the van and opened the rear doors to give the mayor's men access to the shipment. He no sooner had the doors opened than he took notice of Stout standing in the doorway of the garage. He was accustomed to seeing Stout during the drops, but tonight the look on the man's face clearly said he wanted to have a word with Ross alone. He didn't hesitate; he simply walked up to Stout and gave him a half-hearted smile.

"I take it you want to see me?" he asked.

Mason Stout gave his typical Cheshire Cat grin. "That's what I like about you, Berry. So very perceptive. Come on inside; it will take only a moment of your time, and then you can be on your way."

Ross turned back to the van and held up one finger to Mike Biela, indicating he would be right back. Mike nodded at him, and Ross followed the mayor inside. He had never actually been inside the mayor's mansion at all, and he made it a point to take things in, even though the area was obviously only for shipping and receiving.

Mason stopped and turned to Ross. "I insist that you be more dependable when it comes to contacting me before our connection each week," he began. "You understand that I have people whom I must answer to as well, don't you?"

"Of course, Mayor," Ross confirmed. "I apologize. I have had a lot going on, and it just slipped my mind today."

Stout chuckled and began to pace. "Not good enough, Ross. You see, we have been working together long enough that I expect you to be on top of your game at all times. It seems to me that your little 'pony games' have you distracted, and if this is going to be a problem, well, I'm sure I can find someone else who will be more responsible and dependable. Either get it under control or step back, do you understand? If you were as smart as you look, you'd lay off the horses and save some money. Get your act together, man."

Ross' heart began to pound. How did Mayor Stout know he played the horses? He never mentioned it to him; the last thing he needed was to have the man who paid him to know his bad habits. He was very surprised to learn that Stout knew. It gave him a huge jolt of the creeps.

"Who…?"

Mason Stout held up his hand. "Never mind how I know about your little addiction. Do you really expect me to employ people without knowing every little thing about them? You must take me for a fool, Ross Berry."

"No, sir. I…"

"I don't want any more words from you," Mason interrupted. "What I want is just what I said: reliability. So, I will expect consistent behavior from you from here on out. Understood?"

"Yes sir."

Stout put his hand down and nodded. "Good, good. Here is your money. Be a good boy, now; I will talk to you next Thursday, then."

The two men returned to the garage, where Mike sat waiting nervously. The men who had been unloading the truck were gone, as were the coolers. Ross was relieved; he was more than ready to get Mike back to Emmaus and take care of business for himself. He had to come back tomorrow to drop off the refrigeration units to the rental place, and if all went well, he would be picking up his winnings at the same time.

He jumped in the van and reversed out of the garage, saying nothing to his partner. It wasn't until they were pulling on the freeway and heading north that any words were spoken at all. It seemed that curiosity was getting the best of Mike.

"What was that all about?"

Ross was quiet for a moment. "Have you spoken to Stout at all on your own? For any reason?"

"No," Mike said. "Why would you think I did that? The guy gives me the creeps, too, Ross. If I have my way, I'll never have to talk to him alone. Why?"

Ross merged into traffic. "Let's just say he knows some things about me that he shouldn't. Made me kinda nervous, that's all."

"Well, he didn't learn nothing from me."

With that, Mike leaned his head back and put a cigarette in his mouth. He lit it up, and Ross turned on the radio to avoid any further conversation. Soon, he would have Mike home, and he could take care of his own business. Good thing his bookie was functional on a twenty-four-hour-a-day basis.

Ross Berry gave the van some gas, and as the van accelerated he began to relax.

∞

Mayor Mason Stout stood watching his men load the blood into the massive refrigerator at his home. Tomorrow morning every container but one would be shipped out and given to the Loved Ones in his sector. All of them but one, that is, and that one would stay with him. He didn't intend to wait for tomorrow to indulge in his own goods, though. After a moment he stepped forward, took one of the containers by the plastic handle attached to it, and left the area for his own private quarters.

It was important to always sample the goods. At least, that was his motto.

When he was alone, he removed one of the bags of blood from the container. Utilizing the tube attached to the bag, he poured himself a glass of the rich, red liquid of life. The glass equaled exactly one-seventh of his week's rations, and he had one every night. He then proceeded to refrigerate all of it.

He waved the glass under his nose the way a connoisseur might do with fine wine. The powerful metallic aroma put a smile on his face, and he closed his eyes with pleasure. Stout waited only a moment before putting the rim of the glass to his lips and taking a long, leisurely drink of the much-needed substance within.

Oh, it was Heavenly, if indeed there was a Heaven! It was like this every week; Mason was always either very low on blood or completely out by the time Ross Berry arrived with his shipment. This particular week he happened to be completely out, and he had been beside himself waiting for their arrival.

But there was a very shiny side to this coin: Ira Stone was going to be pleased indeed. The blood was so fresh and very, very rich. All of the Loved Ones who would receive in his sector were going to be satisfied, and hopefully, this would get Ira to ease up on him a bit, not to mention the fact that it would please the Dark Father to no end as well.

Mason Stout turned on his stereo system, and

classical music suddenly flooded the room. He sat in a recliner and put his feet up. There he stayed, sipping his blood and reveling in the sound of rushing waves which filled his ears with each drink as the life rejuvenated inside of him. He would live forever, and nothing in the world made him happier than that knowledge.

By the time he was finished, he was so wide-awake and super-sensitive to all that was around him that he knew he would be up for hours to come. Mason stood and rinsed out his glass in the small sink at the bar, then he picked up the telephone receiver and quickly dialed a number.

"Hello, Lewis," he said when his driver answered the phone on the other end. "Bring me a blonde. I think that tonight I would like one with smaller breasts than usual." He paused. "Wonderful. She sounds perfect. I will expect you soon."

Time to shower. His company would be coming in no time. He looked forward to spending the night giving pain and indulging his perversions. There was nothing like living under the gift, nothing at all.

# CHAPTER 5

Mike Biela woke with a start and looked at the clock beside his bed: one thirty in the afternoon.

At first, the time didn't really register to the lazy man. As a matter of fact, he very nearly closed his eyes and snuggled back into the bed. But then it hit him: it was Thursday once again. There had been no call from Ross telling him to get out of bed and get ready to head to Philly.

Mike sat up straight, his heart pounding. Had he missed the call? He ran across the room and grabbed his cell phone from the top of his broken-down dresser, where it sat while it charged; no missed calls.

What was going on? Mike pulled up Ross's number in his contact list and hit the call button. He put the phone's speaker on so he could dress as he talked. He was just pulling on his dirty blue jeans when Ross' number began to ring. It rang five times and went to voicemail.

"You've reached Ross Berry. You know what to do."

Mike turned off the speaker and put the phone to his ear. "Ross, it's Mike. Where are you? I waited for your call," he lied. "I'm ready to hit the road, and I'll be in the parking lot waiting. See you in a bit."

He hung up and finished dressing, then lit a cigarette, grabbed his phone and wallet, and headed out the door, locking up behind him. Mike took a seat on a small set of steps next to the drive, so he could see the cars that drove by. With his phone in his hand, watching the screen for calls, he smoked and waited. Even though he really didn't believe anything was wrong, he did have a sinking feeling in the pit of his stomach; this was not normal behavior for his longtime friend. Even when they were young, Ross had been the punctual and creative one, the one who not only came up with their shady gigs but also made sure they followed through on each and every one of them on time. What was going on?

After a short while, he looked at the clock on his phone: five minutes to two. Where was Ross? Now, the fact was that Mike truly had nothing to do with the deals which he was involved in, but he was beginning to get pretty nervous, nonetheless. He knew that they delivered to a bigwig, and he also knew that there was potential for pretty painful consequences for Ross if they screwed up, so what was going on? He redialed Ross' number, and it went to voicemail once again, but this time it didn't ring at all.

"Hey, man," he said anxiously. "I hope you're okay. We need to get this show on the road, dude. Call me."

At this point, Mike's level of anxiety was slowly rising, and he began to pace. He knew that he really didn't have to worry; any consequences suffered would not come back on him. After all, this was Ross' gig all the way. But yet he couldn't help but be concerned for his friend. He knew Ross well, and he knew that Ross needed every dime of that weekly paycheck just like he did. It was also very much unlike his friend to blow off responsibilities. The guy could hardly stand it when others did it; Ross Berry just didn't have it in him to be consistently irresponsible.

After another fifteen minutes, Mike called his friend's number once again. This time, when it went to voicemail, he told the recording that he would be waiting inside and to honk when he gets there. As he walked back to the door to his tiny studio apartment, his eyes continued to scan the cars passing on the street. Where was Ross?

Since he didn't have a television set, Mike spent the rest of the afternoon with the radio on, walking in and out of the apartment and looking up and down the street. He continued to try his friend's number countless times, to no avail, and finally, he broke down and walked to a convenience store up the block. He picked up a cheap twelve-pack of beer and a package of generic cigarettes with his last twenty bucks. He decided that, if he wasn't going on the run to Philly, it was safe to catch a little buzz. Maybe he would even do his dirty dishes; they had been begging for it for two weeks, and they stank really bad.

Mike Biela fell asleep on his hide-a-bed with a country and western song pumping out of the small clock radio, and as of nine o'clock that night he still had gotten no word from the only friend he had in the world.

∞

On the same day, Thursday, in Philadelphia, Mayor Mason Stout was just finishing up a meeting with his advisor for the pending race for governor. It was around two thirty in the afternoon when the man finally left his office, and Stout was immensely relieved. He had yet to get a call from Ross Berry telling him everything was a go, and he was getting increasingly angry at the fact. When the so-and-so finally did bring the goods to him that evening, Stout was going to see to it he got a bit of a whooping. Maybe that would knock a bit of sense into him.

Mason made sure, for the tenth time, that the ringer of his cellular phone was on high. He turned up the television in his office so he could listen to the news while he put his signature on some paperwork. It would help keep him from staring at the clock and phone every minute if he kept himself busy, and the paperwork needed to be in by the day's end anyway.

As he read things over and signed the stack of papers, he kept one ear tuned to the goings-on in Philadelphia and the rest of the world. Mostly he wasn't even listening. At least, he wasn't until the announcer began talking about the finding of the dead body of a man. Something about it gripped Stout's attention right away, and he knew to drop his pen and tune in to what was being said.

"The body of a man was found on the banks of the Delaware River this morning by a group of teens," the anchorman began, his voice all business. "According to Philadelphia police, the body of Ross Henry Berry, 36, of Emmaus, was found partially concealed by leaves and other debris. The man was beaten and stabbed repeatedly, though the exact cause of death is unknown at the current time. If anyone knows Berry or has information regarding this murder, Philadelphia police ask that they call the station with any and all leads. Back to you, Chris…"

Mason was still holding his pen in his hand, but it dropped immediately to the desk as soon as he heard Berry's name.

Beaten to death and stabbed, huh? Mason thought. Well, Ross Berry, this is what you get when you tinker around with bookies and lowlifes and play the ponies. Stout could only assume his horse had lost, but, of course, it was just an assumption. For all Stout knew, he had simply been robbed. Ah, heck, he supposed he would never know what really happened, but that was the least of his concerns now. The members of the Family in his sector needed their rations, and they needed them fast. To come out from under the umbrella of the gift would mean being dragged down kicking and screaming, for all the Loved Ones.

Now he had to figure out how to come up with the product for the Loved Ones. Just thinking about the issue piqued his concern to the point that he knew his paperwork would not get done right then. He needed to find out who Berry had been getting the product from, but he was at a loss as to how to go about doing that. What was the guy's name that Ross always had in his company? Mark? Mitch? Mike? Yes, it was Mike. Mike Biela.

Mason picked up his telephone and dialed Ira Stone's number. It rang only one time before Stone picked up. His voice sounded irritated and edgy.

"It's about time, Mason," he greeted the mayor. "I assume all is a go in your sector?"

Stout cleared his throat and closed his eyes. "Ira, it seems I have a bit of a problem."

"Imagine that," the man responded. "Do you know how busy I am? You would think that the mayor of one of the most major cities in the US would have his act together, wouldn't you? I am rapidly losing patience with you, Mason, and so is the Dark Father."

Stout ignored his snide comments. "Ira, it seems my provider has been found murdered along the Delaware River."

He was met with silence. After a long moment Ira replied, "Murdered? Are you sure?"

"I'm more than sure," Stout said. "It was just on the news. Police were able to identify him and everything. I have a solution, I believe, but I am not sure how to move forward."

"Continue," Stone said.

Mason cleared his throat yet again. "As you know, Berry was always in the company of another man, a sidekick of sorts. If I can track the man down, I can put him to use; he won't resist, I am sure. But as you know, I cannot proceed without your express permission."

"Well, you have it!" Stone was obviously furious. "What are you waiting for, Stout? Get on it right away! You simply don't have time to waste, understand?"

Mason Stout hung up the phone without saying goodbye. He sat there in silence for a few minutes, considering his next move. Well, the first obvious thing was to track down this Mike Biela. With such short notice, he had no choice but to seek out the only other person familiar with Ross Berry's connection. Mason let his mind drift to what his consequences would be if he didn't figure things out right away, and the thoughts made him shiver. No one, not even the most powerful of vampires, wanted to in any way defy the Dark Father, even if they were defiant at heart.

Stout picked up his phone once again and began to dial.

# CHAPTER 6

Thursday, Friday, and part of Saturday passed without Mike Biela getting any word from his friend Ross Berry. All day Thursday the man worried about his pal. On Friday he began to think that maybe Ross had an accident or had been arrested. But by the time he woke Saturday, after getting very little sleep, he was simply pissed. He simply couldn't believe the man wouldn't try to send word as to his whereabouts by then, and he chalked it up to blatant disrespect. He figured they weren't as good friends as Mike had thought they were.

He slept so little for that two-and-a-half-day period that he actually got quite a bit done around his tiny little abode. For the first time since he had lived there, his place was literally spotless; the bed was made, the dishes were clean, and the dusting and vacuuming had been taken care of as well. He laughed when he thought what his mother would think if she were to see the place; she would have taken his temperature right away. He had even walked up the block to the laundromat and managed to clean every bit of clothing and linens he owned, which wasn't much. He had truly managed to make that change from his last twenty-dollar bill go pretty far.

But now, at three on Saturday afternoon, he was just pissed. He had called the hospitals and jails in both Emmaus and Philly, to no avail, and he now had an irritating habit of checking his phone every thirty seconds. He was at the point that, even if Ross did get in touch with him, he would do nothing more than tear him a new butt and threaten to call both their friendship and working relationship off for good. He didn't deserve this, no matter what, and he refused to accept it. It was no way to treat a friend, to make him worry.

At three thirty, Mike put a TV dinner in the microwave: Salisbury steak with bland mashed potatoes and corn. He certainly wasn't going to starve to death, angry or not. Ross Berry wasn't worth that kind of stress. So, he leaned against the counter of the kitchenette, fork in hand, and watched the microwave as though he were watching a very intense television show.

Just when there was exactly thirty seconds left on the timer, someone knocked hard on his apartment door.

Mike jumped slightly and turned toward the door. His blinds were drawn so he couldn't see who was there, but he wasn't used to visitors. To be honest, he found it extremely unnerving when unexpected guests dropped by, probably because they never did. Knowing the things he had done in the past, and even in the present, it wouldn't surprise him at all to find the cops on his doorstep at any given time. For all he knew, Ross got popped and gave him up to Johnny Blue as well.

The microwave beeped, and the knock came again, harder and more persistent this time. Mike turned the timer to the off position and opened the door so the meal could cool. He put the fork on the counter and slowly and warily headed for the door.

"Hold your horses!" he shouted. "Who is it, anyway?"

"Mr. Biela," said a strong, firm voice. "It is Mason Stout. I need to speak with you right away."

Mike stood there, his eyes wide and his mouth open. Mason Stout? The mayor? What was he doing there? Suddenly Mike thought he got it: Stout must have done Ross in, and now he was here to take care of Mike and get rid of the loose ends. His heart was pounding, and he was looking frantically around his apartment. For what, though? He had no weapons, and there was certainly no way to escape.

"Wh-wh-what do you want?" he stammered.

There was a pause, then that voice again. "I think I made that abundantly clear, Mr. Biela. I need to speak with you… right away!"

Now the man sounded agitated. Mike began to pace. Should he let him in? Should he tell the man to hit the road? It was broad daylight; certainly Stout wouldn't try to harm him in the middle of a Saturday afternoon.

"What do you want with me? Where's Ross?"

Another pause. "If you let me in, I can tell you where your friend is. Don't worry, Mr. Biela; I don't mean you a bit of harm. As a matter of fact, I have a business proposition for you."

Now Mike stopped pacing. A business proposition? What had happened to Ross? Why was this guy at his door, anyway? Mike's stomach was all aflutter with butterflies, and his hand was shaking violently.

"Hold on," he said loudly. He walked to the nightstand next to his hide-a-bed and lit his last cigarette. He supposed he should let the guy in and listen to what he had to say. After all, he was stone-cold broke; he could certainly use the money if that's what the proposition involved.

Mike took a long drag off the cigarette and went to the door. He flipped the deadbolt and undid the chain, then opened the door a crack. Mason Stout stood there with some guy in a black chauffer's uniform. He was tapping his foot impatiently, and when Mike opened the door, he exhaled with annoyance.

"Well," he said snidely. "Are you going to let me in or not? And please, keep your stinking smoke out of my face."

At first, Mike just stared at him through narrow eyes, assessing the possibilities of the situation, but it didn't take him long to realize the fact of the matter: the only way to find out why, and how, the man was at his door was to let him in. Not only that, the guy looked a little green around the gills, and his forehead was sweaty. What if he had some kind of flu or something that was catching? It didn't matter. The guy was the mayor of Philly; if he gave anything to Mike, he would sue.

He stood back and held the door open. "Come on, then. Hope you don't expect a cold beverage or anything. I can't seem to get a hold of Ross, so I'm pretty well flat busted."

Mason Stout entered the grimy apartment, his driver right on his heels. He looked around the place with an air of distaste. With a shiver of disgust, he turned to Mike.

"I'd ask to sit down, but I'm sure I prefer to stand."

Mike grunted and began to make his way back to his TV dinner. "I'm sure. What do you want, Mr. Mayor? Or should I be asking how you found me?"

Stout watched as the man pulled the dinner out of the microwave and removed the plastic wrap. When Mike began to stir the potatoes, Mason gave his driver a look, and the man rolled his eyes in response. Mike took no notice of any of the silent exchange.

"You could ask," Mason replied. "My answer would be to say that I find whoever I want when I want them. That is especially easy for a man in my position. Asking what I want is indeed the more appropriate question. So, did you… 'off' Ross Berry, Mr. Biela?"

Mike turned to him, amused. "Me? 'Off' Ross?" Now he laughed in earnest, but he stopped abruptly as Stout's words sank in. "What do you mean, 'off'?"

Mason studied him briefly. "You don't know? How very interesting. Your business partner, Mr. Berry, was found murdered by the Delaware River. I heard about it on the television news on Thursday." Stout cast his eyes over the small, shabby space that Mike called home. "I guess it would be hard for you to watch the television news without a… television."

"I guess." Mike had forgotten the meal now and was standing, dumbfounded, staring at the well-dressed political figure in his apartment. "You said he was murdered?"

Stout nodded. "Yes, that is what I said."

Mike looked down at the floor and mumbled, "Must've been the bookies."

"Ah, yes!" Mason's eyes lit up in his pale face. "Must have been the bookies! I agree! But that is neither here nor there, now, is it?"

Mike Biela found himself suddenly very agitated with the man. He was actually trying to hold back tears; Ross had been his friend, the only one he really had. He had also been his sole means of income. Now he would have to think about getting a real job, and that truly sucked.

After a brief moment, he looked Stout in the face. "So why are you here and what do you want? If you're finished taunting me over Ross' death, I would like to be alone."

Stout began to pace. "Why am I here and what do I want…"

"Do you have to repeat everything I say?"

Mason stopped and shot a glare at the insect of a man that stood before him. He had the sudden urge to knock the little jerk across the room, but his need got the better of him. "When I communicate, I like to chew on the words and let them become a part of me. There is no better way to accomplish that than through the process of repetition, Mr. Biela. However, I don't owe you an explanation of any kind, especially when I am here to offer you something of great benefit."

Something about the way he spoke, the sternness of his voice, gave Mike a start. His TV dinner was forgotten, and he made his way to his hide-a-bed, where he sat down and glanced longingly at his empty cigarette pack.

"Well? Why are you here?"

Stout came a bit closer to him. "As you may or may not be able to tell, the lack of product, which Berry supplied, has caused members of my family and me to feel a bit… ill."

"What, do all of you have some kind of blood disease or something?"

A smile curved over the man's lips. "How astute of you. Yes, something like that. I have come to make a business proposal. You know the connection which Mr. Berry used to acquire the product, yes?"

Mike nodded but kept his mouth shut.

"No worries, Mr. Biela," he continued. "I don't expect you to divulge your source. I only want to hire you to replace Mr. Berry. That is all."

Suddenly, any grief Mike felt for Ross faded like fog in the morning sun at dusk. Dollar signs began to float through his brain, and sounds like those of a cash register began to fill his ears. It didn't matter that he had never even had a conversation with the guy from BioDonor. Michael Biela had never been beyond introducing himself and proceeding when it needed to be done.

His mind was racing in a thousand different directions: he was adding up the money he didn't have, having an introductory conversation with Vincent Brodsky, and buying a new car all at the same time in his mind. Stout could see that the man was temporarily in la-la land, and he let the guy fantasize for a minute. Sometimes, when good fortune struck, it was best to let the receiver revel, if only for a moment. But Mason Stout didn't have to wait long.

"You want me to take care of business for you?"

Stout nodded vigorously. "Absolutely. I would pay you the entire three thousand which I gave to Mr. Berry every week, plus I would give you the fifty thousand required for each weekly purchase, supplemented with funds for the necessary cooling units. All you need to do is exactly as you have been doing, but you would take the wheel, so to speak."

"I don't have a vehicle, you see," Mike said, his heart falling. "I guess it's not going to work."

Mason Stout groaned with impatience. "Good! Very well. I will supply you with the needed transportation. Call it an 'employee bonus.'

The problem is I need you to get right on this. The 'illness' my family suffers from does not give us much more time before our circumstances become quite... dire... indeed. Well?"

Mike stood, feeling one-hundred-percent better right away. "I'll do it. Do I start Thursday?"

This time when Stout laughed it was sinister and a bit angry. "Did you not hear what I said, little man? I am ill! My Loved Ones are ill! I will need you to get on this immediately!"

"But the vehicle…"

Stout groaned. "The vehicle will be here within the next three hours. In the meantime, get the job lined up! Reserve the cooling units and begin to get your act together. I need the product by Monday at the very latest; I do understand the short notice, and we have enough of what we need to stretch it out until then, but no later. Do you understand?"

Mike just stood there nodding dumbly.

"Fine," Stout said. He gave his driver a curt nod, and the man produced a large, thick envelope. "Here is the money. I must warn you: I wouldn't try to run any kind of scam or 'hustle' on me. I have connections you couldn't possibly imagine. Get on things today, and if you succeed, I will make it well worth your while for coming through on a dime. You will receive a bonus."

Mike took the envelope. "I am on it, Mr. Stout. Right away."

"Good, good." Mason handed a small business card to Mike. "Here is my contact information. Once you get the vehicle and have reached your connection let me know immediately where things stand." He walked to the door, his driver right behind him as usual. "I expect to hear from you soon."

With that, the two men were out the door, closing it almost silently behind them.

When they were gone, Mike opened the envelope to see the stack of cash inside, three thousand of which was his, free and clear. He did a quick dance around the room before gaining his composure. It was time for him to get his act together. He would be driving to Philadelphia that evening to talk to Vincent Brodsky, no matter what.

# CHAPTER 7

The same Thursday that Mason Stout became aware of Ross Berry's demise, Vincent Brodsky had run into a bit of an issue of his own, unbeknownst to Mike Biela.

Brodsky had been waiting that evening for the two men to come to pick up the weekly shipment, just as he always did. But things that evening were as far from the 'usual' as they could be. It seemed that everything took a very nerve-wracking turn, and it was going to prove to be a terrible one in the long run for everyone involved.

He stood there, at the back, watching and waiting for that white van. Time passed, and instead of the van coming, the only thing that came was the deepening darkness of the night. It was enough to make Brodsky tear the flesh from alongside his fingernails. He paced a bit around the rear door, but he mostly remained where he needed to be; he couldn't afford to miss that fifty thousand; he had a little drug problem that dictated this to him clearly.

At last, around eight thirty, he saw the headlights of a car pulling around to the back. He breathed a sigh of relief, but when the vehicle came into view, it was not Berry's van. Instead, it was Raina Gall, the nurse, and the director of BioDonor, Melvin James. They pulled right up to the back door, and they both got out of the car laughing loudly; the two were obviously drunk, as they were staggering, arm in arm, to the rear door that he was waiting by. What happened to not mixing work and play, Mr. James?

What were they doing there? Brodsky ran for the refrigerator to close and lock the unit, even as Melvin James was unlocking the back door. As he fumbled with the lock clumsily, he could hear the back door open, and James told Raina to hurry and get her wallet so they could rejoin the pub crawl before it was too late.

He was caught red-handed, standing there, frantically trying to lock the refrigerator.

"What are you doing, Brodsky?" Melvin James asked in a loud, angry voice.

Vincent spent a full ten minutes stuttering and tripping over his own tongue as he tried to justify why there were Styrofoam coolers of blood stacked and waiting to go. But no answers came to him. James confiscated his refrigerator key and sent him packing that night without even letting him clean out his desk. He was told to come back Saturday when the donation center was closed. Then he was to clean out his desk and leave the keys to the building. If anything was missing or the keys were not there for Raina on Monday, the law would be at his door and charges would be pressed. Vincent just couldn't have that; he couldn't face withdrawal and detox while behind bars. The thought overwhelmed him almost to the point of tears.

Now it was seven thirty on Saturday, and Brodsky was sitting in his old office, packing a box with every last worldly possession he had there at BioDonor. He couldn't believe this had happened, and he was deep into the throes of depression over it. He was tempted to torch the place, but he knew he wouldn't. It was all a pipe dream consisting of his desire for revenge, but the loss of his job was his own fault. He was lucky he wasn't heading to jail, and he knew it.

Suddenly Brodsky heard the chime coming from the reception area. The chime signified that someone was at the main door and was ringing for service. Melvin James had it hooked up five years prior for the slow days when only one nurse was working, before business had picked up so rapidly. It was hardly ever used, and Brodsky expected no one. He was not only surprised by the sound; he was very confused. Who would that be?

Brodsky made his way to the front. He peered through the glass double doors to see a man and a woman. Both of them were wearing long white lab coats, and as he neared he could see that both of them were marked 'GenetiLabs.' He recognized the name as a medical science lab across town that conducted medical experimentation. He could care less; whatever they wanted would have to wait until Melvin James came in on Monday or hired a new manager. The pair waiting on the other side of the door were certainly not his problem, and he refused to let them be.

He flipped the lock and looked at them both. "Yes?"

"We are here for a meeting with Mr. James," the man said.

Brodsky shrugged and offered them a sneer. "He won't be here until Monday; you'll have to come back then."

At that exact moment a black, shiny panel van pulled into the main drive. At first, it seemed it was going to pull around back, but it paused, then pulled right up to the front. Was it Melvin James?

All three of them watched, but to Brodsky's shock, the driver's side door opened and out popped Ross Berry's partner, Mike Whatever-his-name-was. Brodsky's eyes grew wide, but he said nothing. After a second he turned to the two GenetiLabs people.

"Uh, look, I have to be out of here within the half-hour," he said nervously. "Maybe you should call Mr. James and figure things out with him, but I can't let you in, or it will be my head."

The two people looked at each other, exasperated. Finally, the woman said, "Maybe you could leave him a message that we were here at the agreed-upon time?"

"Fine, fine," was Brodsky's urgent response.

The two walked away and climbed into a white sedan with 'GenetiLabs' emblazoned on the doors, and after only a second Brodsky watched them speed out of the lot. He turned his attention to Mike. The man was just standing there, watching the sedan leave just like he was.

"What are you doing here?" Vincent asked.

Mike jumped slightly, startled out of his reverie by

Brodsky's voice. "Oh, hey. I need to talk to you. Ross has passed on, unfortunately, and his customer wants me to pick up where he left off."

Brodsky almost guffawed. "Well, that's not gonna work. I got fired when you guys didn't show last Thursday because my boss showed up while I was waiting. He caught me with all the… the product. Now I'm unemployed, he took my refrigerator key, and even if I weren't fired, I'd be done for good with the likes of you."

With that, Vincent closed the glass door and locked it, walking away as if Mike didn't exist. Mike stood staring at the man as he disappeared into the rear of the BioDonor building. Now, what the heck was he going to do? He had no connections in the 'illegal blood trade.'

Mike began to walk back to his van, and suddenly it hit him: GenetiLabs! They must be another blood bank! He knew he couldn't just call them up and offer them money for black market stuff. As he got comfortable in the van and started it up, he continued to think. Something inside of him told him that this could be exactly the break he needed, but how?

No, he thought as he pulled out of the lot. He couldn't just call them up. But he could break into the place. He was a thief way back in the day, after all, and a pretty good one at that. One of his best qualities was lack of fear, not to mention that he had some good skills when it came to window and door locks.

It was too late to proceed without planning, so he

pulled over and went into the Jiffy Stop gas station, where he borrowed their phone book. He looked up the address to GenetiLabs, then started driving to the location to case out the place. He would see what he could see, make a plan, and hit the place tomorrow night. A perfect way to spend a Sunday.

He could feel the old excitement coming back as he drove across town to the location. Not only was it a rush to do a job like this, but to pull in a full fifty-three grand from it was outstanding. After all, he wouldn't be paying for the product he was stealing now, would he? No, he would be pocketing a load of cash, and it would be his, all his. He was beside himself for the first time in years.

Maybe Ross Berry's murder was actually spelling out a brand new beginning for the lowlife Mike Biela.

# CHAPTER 8

Mike Biela lay still on the hide-a-bed in his apartment, his head on his pillow, smoking a cigarette and staring at the ceiling. It was three o'clock on Sunday afternoon, his belly was full, and the beer on his nightstand was good and cold. All he was really doing was passing the time…

He would leave around five for a return trip to Philadelphia. He spent most of the day spending money. He had purchased two lightweight refrigeration units with high inner capacity, along with power adaptors and battery packs. He had them installed inside the spiffy new van that Stout had delivered to him. He also bought forty Styrofoam coolers, much like the ones that had held the blood which he had always picked up with Ross, only slightly different in design. He was ready for the entire transport process, and he had tons of funds left over.

The night before he had cased out GenetiLabs, and it had turned out to be such a shoo-in that he simply couldn't believe his luck. There was an alarm system at both the main and rear entrances to the small building, but it had been obvious that the place was only a fledgling establishment. The windows weren't wired in any fashion, and they had no security guards at all. The windows even had simple locks and frames; Mike knew he could easily remove an entire upper pane, even if the window was locked, and gain access in less than a minute. The thought of his pending success made him smile, and his heart skipped a beat from the pleasure.

He sat up on one elbow and drained his beer, taking notice of the time as he did so: three ten. Why was time passing so slowly? He was ready to go, but it would do no good to become impatient. Instead, Mike stood up and fetched another cold beer from his refrigerator, then returned to his place on the bed. He found himself wishing he had at least thought to buy himself one of those new flat-screen television sets.

Mike spent the next two hours alternating between lying around in his apartment and admiring his van as he smoked in the parking lot. He was especially pleased with the speedy job of installation that was done on his refrigeration units. He had thought of everything; there was no doubt about it. This job was not only fortunate; it was ideal, and so far, he was handling the responsibility of it like a pro. His old buddy Ross would have been proud of him; that was for sure.

Now, all he needed to do was to travel around and find other blood banks or other medical labs that he could rob. It wouldn't be difficult, especially if each one carried a fifty thousand dollar per week paycheck. He would be able to breach the most difficult of security, even if it meant bribing security guards. That kind of thing was easy to do when you pulled in that kind of money. He could offer one of those poor jerks a grand, and they would buckle, and Mike wouldn't even notice he was short on cash from the deal. He loved it!

He toyed around with the idea of moving, which he fully intended to do once he transferred the goods to Stout and his men. The sky was the limit; that was a fact. For the first time in his life, Mike Biela believed he might just be able to get out of the twenty-year slump he had been in, and it felt good. Maybe he could meet a nice girl; he had sure dreamed of it enough. Who knew? Some new threads, a haircut and shave, and he might just have half a chance.

For the last forty-five minutes of his wait, Mike napped lightly. He had set the alarm to wake him at exactly five, but he didn't need it. He was too hopped up to really enjoy a good sleep at all, so at five minutes to five he sat up, wide awake, and turned off his alarm. He grabbed his cigarettes and keys in one deft motion, then went out to the van, locking the door to the apartment behind him. Soon, he was on the road to Philly, whistling along to a classic rock tune on the radio and puffing on a cigarette.

∞

Mike ended up parking in a 'by-the-month' lot located a half-block down from GenetiLabs. He paid for a full month without giving it a thought, then chose a space which afforded him a very generous view of the place. Then it was time for another waiting game; nothing like chain-smoking in silence and staring dully ahead. A couple of times the monotony even caused him to nod out.

He spent the time staring at GenetiLabs and thinking about Ross. He remembered how frustrated he had been over forgetting to call Stout the last time they were together, and the thought made him smile. For a crook, the dude had been down on himself all the time, worrying about being late, worrying about his bookies. If someone hadn't stabbed him to death, the ulcers in his stomach would have killed him for sure. Poor dude. But Mike had to admit it, he missed his friend.

Finally, his time came. The last car in the lab parking lot left, and when it was well out of sight, Mike reached behind his seat. He withdrew two large magnetic panels he had made for the side of his van, which read 'Mitchell's Plumbing and Maintenance.' He looked them over with pride and a smile on his face. Looking inconspicuous was very important, especially when it came to police cruisers on routine patrol. The panels would definitely alleviate any attention that came his way.

He got out of the van and quickly slapped the panels onto the van, then got back in and proceeded to head over to the lab building. Mike drove by twice so he could get a view of both sides of the building; he wanted to be sure he hadn't missed any vehicles that could potentially be out of view, but he saw none. As a matter of fact, with the exception of the lights over the main entrance and some dim inner lighting in the back of the building, the place looked dead. Black as night in the windows, and still as a sleeping baby's nursery.

It was time to move.

He backed up to a solid metal door on the side of the building which read 'Emergency Exit Only.' He knew this door would be rigged up to an alarm, but that didn't bother him. He would be using a window, at least initially. Next, he opened both the rear loading doors on his van, then walked over to the window closest to the van, but farthest from the street. Gloves on, he looked it over carefully with a small penlight between his teeth. Yes, this one will be an easy open, he thought to himself with a smile.

After a quick glance back out to the deserted street, Mike flattened his palms against the glass on the upper pane of the window. He pushed in and up on the pane slightly and immediately felt it give. He smiled but didn't rush. He was too busy making sure no wiring came into view, signifying an alarm he may have missed; nothing. He laughed to himself and kept going. He needed to stop being such a ninny.

Now he gently pushed inward and, just as he expected, the top part of the pane went inward. Mike's fingers quickly and deftly curved around it, catching it and swiftly removing the upper pane from the frame entirely. It was so easy he was afraid to breathe. He turned the pane to the side and silently brought it outside, where he laid it flat on the grass next to the building. Now he was able to wedge his body into the building without any problem whatsoever.

Within thirty seconds, Mike Biela was standing on

the cold tile floor inside of what was obviously a laboratory.

Dim lighting illuminated the room, but only softly. He looked around and gave a low whistle. The place smelled of antiseptic, and everything seemed to be made of glistening stainless steel. Mike didn't know much about blood or labs or science, but he did know what he was looking for: the heavy, sealed door to a walk-in refrigerator.

He found it right away. He almost considered himself lucky that he had come directly into the lab so quickly and efficiently, but he took note right away that the lab spanned the entire length of the building; every window on that side was to the lab. It was too easy.

Right there, in the center of the wall opposite that long line of windows, was the refrigerator door, complete with a large suction-equipped handle. A sign with large black letters taped over the handle read: 'Door Must Remain Open When Unit is Occupied!'

He took hold of the handle and pulled. The seal broke, and the door came open. Mist from the cold unit rushed into the warm lab, giving him a chill. He quickly entered, being certain that the door stayed open behind him.

Mike wasn't sure what he was looking for exactly. After all, he had never seen the actual blood that he and Ross had picked up because it had always been in the Styrofoam coolers. But he soon discovered he had nothing to worry about. Along the far wall, on a large aluminum shelving system, were literally rows and rows of blood in clear plastic bags. Each bag looked to contain about a quart apiece.

He had hit pay dirt, and he had done it with the skill and timing of a true black-market blood dealer.

But there was something which he could not decipher: a large red symbol was printed on each bag. The symbol reminded him of those on the needle disposal containers at doctors' offices and clinics, but he couldn't be sure. Not to mention the fact that they looked a little different somehow. The symbols were on stickers affixed to each bag. He didn't care. It was time to get the coolers in here.

A quick trip out the window and to the van and Mike grabbed coolers, three in each hand. He tossed them through the window and repeated the process five more times. When he had at least thirty-some coolers he decided that was enough; the last few remained forgotten in the van for next time.

Back inside Mike began to load up the coolers with the bags of blood sporting the odd stickers. The only other markings he noticed on the bags were small white stickers marking the blood type and date; all of the dates were recent. Four quart bags fit comfortably into each cooler, and he took each one he filled and stacked it on a clean stainless steel countertop beneath the window. After forty-five minutes, thirty-two filled coolers were neatly stacked, waiting to be put into the van.

That process didn't take long at all. He grabbed them, two at a time, from outside the window, and packed them neatly into his refrigerators. By the time he was finished, he had room in the last fridge to spare, and it made him smile. He closed them up, padlocked each, and quickly returned to the window to replace the pane, wipe it free of smudges, and get the show back on the road.

Now he was taking the back road toward the governor's mansion, smug and very pleased with himself indeed. He flipped his cell open and speed-dialed Stout himself. Stout answered on the first ring.

"Stout."

"I'll be there in twenty minutes, Mr. Mayor," Mike said in a monotonous, business-like tone.

Silence answered him, then a simple, "Good." The line disconnected.

Mike tossed the phone onto the passenger seat and lit a cigarette. He turned the radio up and set the cruise control. He was very pleased. Mason Stout had given him until Monday, and here he was, locked and loaded and ready to go at ten fifteen on Sunday night.

Looked like he had permanent employment.

∞

"Excellent, Mr. Biela."

Mike stood, smiling, as he watched Stout's men unload the truck. It had all gone so smoothly, and all the money was his. He did have one dilemma in the beginning: Stout discovering that he hadn't hooked up with the usual connection. But Mike had a solution to this concern that would make everyone happy: he would simply tell the truth.

Stout clasped him on the shoulder with one hand,

and Mike glanced down at it. The man had unusually long nails, and they were even kind of pointed on the end. Creepy.

"Let's talk, Michael," Stout purred, and gave his shoulder a gentle tug.

Mike followed him into the house and down a short series of tastefully decorated hallways. At last, they turned into a massive office furnished in cherry wood, with high-priced art and antiques. Stout gestured toward a chair situated opposite a large desk and closed the door behind him.

"So," Stout began. "I take it you had an easy enough time convincing Mr. Berry's connection to let you pick up where he left off?"

Mike gave a nervous but determined chuckle. "Not exactly, sir."

Mason sat down at the desk and leaned back, putting his feet on the blotter in a motion that was highly reminiscent of a cat's. "Really? So?"

Mike cleared his throat and picked a piece of imaginary lint off his worn jeans. "I mean, I went to talk to the man, but he told me he was fired on the night Ross didn't show up because he was... he was caught with the goods, and they were ready to move out the door."

"Oh, my." Mason put his feet back on the floor and leaned toward Mike in a conspiratorial manner. "I'm sure you said nothing. So, what did you do?"

"Well, there was another blood company," he began slowly. "They showed up while I was there. They had some kind of meeting with the guy who runs the joint. Anyway, to be honest, I cased their place and I… I robbed it. The extra blood is my gift to you."

Mason Stout immediately broke into a fit of laughter. He was amused and impressed. He honestly didn't know how Mike Biela got his hands on the goods. The important thing was that he did. He admired the fact that the man was an obvious problem solver.

After a long moment, his laughter subsided. "So, I take it you have experience in this sort of venture? I mean, you must have done such a thing in the past?"

Mike's hands were sweating, so he wiped them off on the legs of his jeans. "Listen, Mr. Mayor," he began. "I do have some shady dealings in my past, yes. I had a few… problems which required me to be creative, but those things are behind me. I ran into an issue with the connection, and I used my past experience to eliminate the issue. It's that simple."

"And that, my friend, is good enough for me."

Now Stout stood and began his habitual pacing. "Obviously you will not be able to go back to that site next week. Is it safe to assume that you have another agenda?"

"Absolutely, sir," Mike said firmly, looking the man directly in the eye. "You can count on me."

"Excellent!" He walked to a large portrait of himself which hung over the fireplace. Stout swung the portrait back to reveal a safe, and after punching in a code at lightning pace, he withdrew another envelope. With that, he returned to Mike and handed it to him.

"Here is a ten-thousand-dollar bonus, Michael," he said. "I want you to know that you have so impressed me that I have decided to keep you on for as long as you continue to do so. However, I believe you have settled for less for far too long. It is time for you to find a more suitable place to live, and purchase some more appropriate clothing."

"Thank you, sir," Mike said as he stood.

Stout draped an arm over the man's shoulders. "Now, take care of those details. If you need anything, and I mean anything, to help you meet those goals, call the number on my card. You take care of me, and I take care of you; it's really that simple. I will expect to hear from you by next Thursday morning at the latest. And please, wear something decent. You can see yourself out, yes?"

With that, Mason Stout put Mike Biela into the corridor and closed the office door between them.

Mike stood there, dumbfounded, but only for a short time. Soon he was making his way back down the maze of corridors to the loading area. He was both invigorated and excited. It was time for him to find his next target, but this time he would hit Pittsburgh, he thought.

He wanted to keep things at more of a distance.

# CHAPTER 9

At the same time that Mike Biela was sitting and smoking in the by-the-month parking lot, watching the last car pull out of GenetiLabs, the driver of the car was receiving a call on his cellular phone.

Dr. Quentin Varney was the head of the lab at GenetiLabs, and he was also the head of their current study. Varney had stumbled upon a very specific genetic mutation of the blood which could potentially cure cancer. At least, it was looking more than promising; it seemed like it was going to be a sure thing. The problem was that they had run out of test blood, and as of yet, they had been unable to acquire a contract for a new supply.

He was just pulling out of the lot when his cell chirped twice, rapidly, in succession.

"Quentin Varney."

"Quentin! It's Allen Chandler. Are you still at the lab?"

Quentin flinched. Allen Chandler was the president and head scientist over all of GenetiLabs, and he was a nag of the most supreme kind. Quentin was making astronomical progress on the mutation, but it seemed he could still count on annoying calls from Chandler at least three times a day. Usually, it was regarding perfecting the mutation for FDA approval, but as of late it had been in regards to whether or not Quentin had managed to find new blood.

"No, Allen," he answered, trying to force himself to sound more chipper than he felt. "I'm already almost home." He never felt bad about lying, but if he told the truth and said he had just left, Chandler would want him to turn around and go right back. Chandler didn't want a lab head; he wanted a machine.

"Oh, I see," Chandler replied, his disappointment obvious. "I was just calling to see if you had any word yet from the guy at BioDonor, the one you and Jill Weston were supposed to meet with last night."

Quentin pulled up to a stop light and briefly closed his eyes. "It's Sunday, Allen. He'll be back in tomorrow, I'm sure. I'll make sure to call him in the morning and schedule another meeting. I won't forget, Al. You can depend on me."

"I know," Allen said with a bit of false shame in his voice. "I know I can, Quentin. I don't mean to be such a drag. But you know how important this is to the world. Tell me, how do you think those last samples are, anyway? Is the potency right? How are the animals reacting?"

Quentin gave up and pulled into a PowerPump gas station. He parked in one of the spots in front of the small store and put his sedan in park. "Well, I can tell you that while the potency isn't yet perfect, it is wiping out the cancer cells it confronts with alarming speed. The problem is the side effects the animals are displaying. They are cancer-free, but they are violent, and some of the physical changes are alarming. I will continue my focus on perfecting the potency, and I will also continue the pursuit of new blood, capiche?'

"All right, Quent," Chandler said in a resigned voice. "It's been hard to sleep. I guess I'm a bit of a harper. Oh, by the way, with things as they currently are, how are you destroying the animals?"

"Still using the incinerator, Al."

Allen's sigh was audible. "Good. Guess I'll see you in the morning. Keep me posted on those concerns, will you?"

Quentin ignored the question, but said in a comforting tone, "Have a good night, Al. Get some sleep."

With the call disconnected, Quentin pulled out of the lot and back into traffic. He just wanted to go home, have a nice brandy, and go to bed himself. They were handling everything strictly according to protocol; Allen seriously needed to relax.

The only thing that could stop them now was if someone got a hold of that blood and used it, and that would never happen. Allen Chandler was way too stressed out and impatient. He needed a brandy more than Quentin did.

With that, Quentin Varney put the entire situation out of his mind and headed for home.

Mason Stout sat at the desk in his office enjoying the darkness; the only light in the room was a nice fire in the fireplace.

There were no sounds in the house, but he knew that his men were still arranging the latest shipment in its special place, in a refrigeration unit just off the loading area. They had to categorize and assign the blood to cover every Family member in Stout's sector, including Stout himself. They would be at it until around three in the morning.

Mason had already called Ira Stone and let him know everything was smooth sailing, and Stone had been very pleased indeed. It seemed that, regardless of the loss of Ross Berry and the lack of knowledge as to what the future held for all of the Loved Ones, things were going to turn out beautifully.

Mason was literally beside himself with impatience. It was his responsibility to try the first of the blood out of every shipment, and he just knew, deep inside, that what was to come was going to be very, very special indeed. He could smell the wonderful life liquid through the bag! Not only did it reek of the promise of prolonged life, but it also offered an aroma of spice which he could not quite place, but the strange scent literally made his mouth water with anticipation.

He glanced at the clock on the mantel; oh, it was almost time now. Only one more hour to go. Why couldn't his men hurry and complete their tasks, for Satan's sake?

Stout stood and began to pace, as per usual. Not two minutes passed when there were three sharp raps at his office door. What was left of his heart began to immediately pound with excitement.

"Yes!"

The door opened slightly and his driver, Lewis, poked his head through. He was out of his uniform and was wearing only a khaki-colored work uniform with no distinguishable patches or markings.

"Master Stout, all is loaded and assigned, with all proper labels, just as you require."

Mason smiled broadly. "Already, Lewis?"

The man nodded a single time. "Yes, sir. We all worked together rather smoothly this night."

Lewis closed the door right away, wasting no time in letting the mayor be alone to himself. He had been with Stout for years that could not be counted, and he knew that the time had come for his employer to sample the wares. After all, the sooner that was done, the sooner he would get his own rations.

Mason waited only long enough to be sure that the rest of his staff were out of his way; he hated to go and fetch his trial bag while others were around. He always felt weak and overly excited during that time, and he didn't want them to be able to see the way he felt in his actions. He was sure it was obvious that he felt just like a kid in a candy store, and just as he suspected, that was exactly how he looked to the few who had snuck around and gotten an eyeful.

Ten minutes was all Mason Stout could handle.

He ran from his office, the black satin robe he was wearing flying and flapping behind him. The closer he got to the loading area and the refrigerator, the stronger the smell of the blood behind the door. Its spice tickled his nose so strongly that he could taste it on his tongue. By the time he reached the door to the walk-in refrigerator, he was quite literally out of his mind with the hunger.

Stout flung the door open, and the entire area lit up immediately. Around him, on shelves which covered each of the three large walls in the cube-shaped space, were rows of coolers, more than what Mike Biela had brought. Mason's men had separated the bags and transferred the blood into coolers of their own, each assigned to a different Loved One in the sector. But Mason Stout took notice of none of those.

There on the floor, in a cooler marked 'Mayor Stout', were his rations for the week, and that was the one his eyes were focused on.

With a single long stride, he reached it. He fell to one knee and tore the lid off the cooler, grabbed a bag from the container, and uncapped the tube which protruded from it. It was as if he could not wait to put the thing to his lips.

Normally, each of the Loved Ones would need to ration their bag to last the entire week, meaning approximately one-seventh or less would make up a serving. That serving would empower them, strengthening them for the day and enabling them to live in the sunlight, leading a seemingly normal and productive life amongst the living.

But this time was very different, and Stout was too out of his mind to even recognize it. The scent that filled his nostrils had driven him out of his mind with ravenous desire, and he was no longer in control of himself at all. Every last ounce of self-control which the Dark Father had bestowed was gone, and it was the doing of nothing more than the smell of the blood Mike Biela had brought to him.

Stout put the tube between his lips and began to drink. Right away his ears began to roar deafeningly, and a red fog filled his vision. Any and all sane thoughts in his mind disappeared like a puff of smoke in a brisk wind, and Mason Stout did nothing but drink.

He didn't know how much time had passed when the bag, completely drained, fell to the refrigerator floor between his knees. He simply knelt there, gasping for breath, eyes closed and face turned upward in sheer ecstasy. After only a minute his eyes began to flutter open, and he looked down at the bag.

Mason's first thought upon seeing the empty bag was 'What have I done?', but the thought soon dissipated. An icy chill ran up his spine, down his legs and arms, and over the entirety of his head and face. The tremors took over then, his body beginning to spasm as if he were in the throes of a grand mal seizure.

Stout lay there on the cold floor, thrashing about for what seemed an eternity. Then, suddenly, it stopped, and he lay limp and lifeless, his mind a blank. Suddenly his body gave a violent jerk, and as quickly as he had seized and passed out, Mason awoke again. He opened his mouth and let out a horrifying, blood-curdling scream before sitting straight up and opening his eyes wide.

Suddenly, things were going to change for the Loved Ones of the Dark Father, never to be reversed again.

# CHAPTER 10

Monday morning was drizzly and cold, and the drive to work was hectic and dangerous for Quentin Varney. It seemed that everyone on the road was either angry or asleep at the wheel, putting him on guard the entire drive. It was enough to send him over the edge when it came to his anxiety.

He was always the first to arrive at GenetiLabs, partly because he was a workaholic, but mostly because he was responsible for unlocking the building and getting the proverbial ball rolling. By the time his assistant Jill Weston arrived, as well as the rest of the staff, he would be chest-deep in work and barely even be able to acknowledge any of them. He chalked it up to being nothing more than a hazard of his personal profession.

The sun was just coming up on the horizon when he slid his key into the lock. From there on, Quentin had a very dependable routine: lights on, make coffee in the break room, go into the lab and flip on his own coffee pot, check the temperature on the refrigerator, and fire up the burners he would be using for the day. He did everything in one big circle, ensuring that he didn't forget any detail. The rest of the GenetiLabs staff had come to depend on Quentin's ways so much they took him for granted, and he knew it, but he couldn't care less. None of them could be depended on to even complete a regular daily shift.

With all of his tasks completed in the outer area of the building, Quentin finally unlocked the lab. Briefcase in hand, he flipped the bright overhead lights on and stepped inside. At first, his eyes were on the ground as he stood in the doorway putting his ring of keys into his pocket. Then his eyes went to the coat tree situated about five feet in front of the door. He set his briefcase down and grabbed his white coat. As he began putting it on, he finally took the time to look around.

The refrigerator door was wide open.

Quentin let his lab coat fall to the floor, forgotten. His mind was racing, and his heart was pounding; had he done this? Had he neglected to close the unit when he left the night before? Oh, this would cost him his job! If the refrigerator had been open all night, every single specimen and sample inside would be compromised and therefore destroyed. Without another thought, he raced for the refrigerator.

When he reached the opened unit, he stopped dead in his tracks. Around three-quarters of the treated blood was gone. Shelves were completely bare; an unidentifiable Styrofoam cooler lay on its side, and its lid was across the room. Two bags of treated, mutated blood were broken open and splattered all over the floor. Quentin Varney's mouth simply fell open.

"Son of a…," he muttered under his breath before he turned around and rushed to the phone on his desk in the corner of the room.

Quentin dialed 911 with the receiver up to his ear. Now was not the time to call Allen Chandler; he would do that once the police were notified. Right at that moment, all he was worried about was getting the cops down there as quickly as possible. His mind was spinning as he spoke to the dispatch officer; who in the heck stole blood? But worse than that, the blood that had been stolen was highly volatile and dangerous. It would kill any normal human being in its current state; it was far from being ready, even in the tiniest of amounts.

Once he was assured that the police were coming, and he had been advised to remain in the lab, with the door locked, in case the thieves were still in the building, he hung up the phone. Quentin began to walk around and observe the entire lab to see if anything else had been taken, without touching anything, of course. When he got back to the refrigerator, he stopped and stood, staring at the disastrous mess and shaking his head.

The rats which they were testing the blood on had turned into vile, monstrous little beasts in ways that the layman wouldn't understand. He could barely understand it himself. What, in the name of all that was good and holy, would happen to a human if the same blood began to pump through their veins? The very thought made him shudder, and Quentin was suddenly overwhelmingly nauseous. He ran out of the unit and into the staff lab restroom right next to it. There,

Quentin leaned over the toilet and threw up every last drop of coffee he had ingested since he woke up, then he dry-heaved until his stomach ached and his muscles hurt.

"Dr. Varney?"

The voice came from the lab. Quentin wiped his mouth quickly on his sleeve and stood up, flushing the toilet as he did so.

"I'm in the bathroom here," he hollered. "I'll be right out!"

He sucked a couple of handfuls of water from the tap out of the palm of his hand, swished them around in his mouth, and spit them back into the sink. After quickly grabbing a brown paper towel for his mouth he left the bathroom. Two male uniformed officers stood there, hands on their guns, waiting to see his face.

"Yes," he said. "I'm Dr. Varney. I'm the head of the lab here at GenetiLabs. Unfortunately, we have had a break-in."

The first officer, a man with the name Harding on his nametag, said, "Right. So, this is the only area that you know of so far that was violated?"

"Um, yes sir," Quentin replied. "I've been through the entire building, and as far as I can tell, this was it."

The other officer, named Fredericks, chimed in. "Anything missing?" He whipped out a small spiral notebook and pen and flipped it open.

"I'm afraid so, and it's sort of a dangerous situation, to put it mildly." Quentin could feel the beginnings of a headache coming on; his hand went to his right temple and began to gently massage.

"Well?" Fredericks asked.

Quentin gestured toward the refrigerator with his free hand. "In here." He made his way to the unit with the officers following him. "Blood, and a lot of it. You see, that's the problem."

Fredericks was now standing in the doorway jotting in his pad. Harding said, "Besides the obvious fact that it's gone, what's the problem? What do you mean, 'that's the problem'?"

"Well," Quentin began slowly, "the blood was undergoing testing and mutation processes. It was part of a cancer treatment study and was highly volatile. Tell me, have you ever heard of people stealing blood before?"

Fredericks turned to him. "I've never dealt with a blood theft personally, but I have heard about such a thing. How much was stolen approximately, Dr. Varney?"

Quentin shrugged, his head beginning to pound harder. "I would have to say around eight gallons or so."

Both officers stared at him. "Eight gallons?"

Quentin nodded and let out a long, laborious sigh. "Yep."

"And it was like this when you came into work?" Harding asked. "I mean, did you disturb anything?"

"Other than starting the coffee pot, opening the refrigerator door, and calling you on the telephone, I touched absolutely nothing."

Fredericks was writing furiously now, but Harding continued to confer with Quentin. "We are going to have the crime scene unit come down and dust for prints and check over things for any other evidence. Standard procedure, you know."

"So," Quentin asked after a quick nod of confirmation at Harding. "In the cases you know of, the ones with stolen blood, do you have any idea what the thieves may have used the blood for?"

"Sure," Harding said. "For sale on the black market, of course. Underground medical facilities and such across the border and overseas buy stuff like this all the time. Unlicensed physicians always have their radars out for stuff they couldn't otherwise get their hands on… body parts, surgical supplies, blood, and the like."

"Oh," Quentin groaned.

Harding raised his eyebrows. "What? That bad? What will this blood do other than killing a person?"

"Well, I could show you, but it would compromise the scene," Quentin said, his head pounding full force now. "Let's just say yes, it would kill them. Listen, go ahead and do what you have to do. I have to call the president of the company and get him down here. He's going to crap his pants."

Harding nodded and took his radio out of his belt to call for the crime scene unit. "Use another phone," he said. "We are going to need to seal off your lab, Doctor. Sorry."

Quentin nodded glumly and headed out of the lab. He needed an aspirin, but now was not the time to worry about himself. He went to the front desk and picked up the reception phone, so he could call Allen Chandler. His briefcase, with his cell in it, was still in the lab. He had left it right where it was; no big deal, after all.

As Chandler's cell rang, Quentin sank down into the receptionist's chair and put his head in his other hand. His stomach was doing flip-flops, and he thought he might vomit again. How could this have happened?

It was going to be one unforgettable day, no matter how things went.

∞

Something was just not right; in fact, something was very, very wrong.

Mason Stout had begun feeling uneasy only seconds after coming to his senses on the floor of the refrigerator in the loading dock, and ever since that moment, he had chills and severe pain in all of his muscles and joints. Even his mouth and gums had been aching and stinging unbearably. He had rushed back to his office, where he had been sitting on the floor in the darkness, curtains drawn to keep the light out ever since.

It was now seven thirty on Monday morning.

His temper was short, and he found that even the slightest sound irritated him to anger beyond belief. Even the sound of his staff beginning to bustle here and there in the mansion was almost more than he could bear, and around seven he had stuck his head out of his office and screamed for them to leave the general area until further notice. He called his assistant and canceled his entire day, then shut the ringer off on his office phone and took the position he was in now.

He was in terrible pain. He didn't know why, and for some reason, he didn't relate it to his consumption of the blood at all. In his mind he was simply... ill. Mason figured that, since the Dark Father had given his kind so many permissions and freedoms, perhaps he was becoming one of the living again, or at least like them. He figured he was ill.

But now something new was happening. His eyeteeth, the ones which had subsided from their past prominent state when the promises had been made real by the Dark Father, were now coming to a sharp point once again. He realized it when he bit into his own tongue and grazed it. He felt no pain, but he did feel the skin tear, and it was enough to send him reeling into a state of confusion.

That wasn't all. As he sat in the darkness, his head on fire and his eyes burning, he was beginning to envision things. Things which had long been over. Murder, mayhem, and the ecstasy of draining the life out of human beings by sucking it right from their bodies. The visions made him erect, and he even began to lust sexually after every woman on his staff who walked, tiptoeing, by his office door. He could smell them. He could smell both their blood and their musk, and it was driving him mad with a double desire that he could not quell with his mind.

But he still had a bit of his mind about him, and it

told him to stay put, not to chase his desires, at least not yet. The sun was shining outside, and it promised to continue to shine brightly throughout the day. The very thought of its powerful rays made his skin hurt.

He could remember a time, countless months and years ago, when he had to hide from the sun to survive. But it wasn't just he who had to do this, it had been all of the Loved Ones. That is until the Dark Father had bestowed his gifts. Now it seemed that the memory of those times was upon him full force, to the point that he couldn't even stand the thought of those recollections.

It seemed, for some reason, that his past had suddenly and powerfully become his present. He didn't know that for sure, but with each passing second, it was becoming more and more obvious. Had the love of the Dark Father suddenly leave him? What had he done to deserve that? Mason Stout had conducted things in his assigned sector just as he always had. He was not only confused but bitter with anger.

His skin began to crawl, and his ears picked up the distant voice of one of the females in the house, likely one of his kitchen or housekeeping staff. He plugged his ears up with his fingers and closed his eyes tight; he couldn't bear the way even the sound of her voice made him feel. He was powerless to quell the thoughts that the sound planted in his mind, the thoughts which he was powerless to act on because of the sun.

The only thing he was truly aware of, outside of himself and his misery, was the fact that everyone in his home and on his staff were members of the Family.

Why was he the only one unable to face the day?

But all Mason Stout could do was sit and wait. He couldn't even pick up the telephone to contact the Dark Dominant, Ira Stone, and beg him for his help. The thought of any sound entering his skull made his head feel as though it would explode.

No, he could do nothing but wait.

# CHAPTER 11

By three o'clock that afternoon, the city of Philadelphia was in the very beginnings of a siege that it was not yet aware of.

Paula Harmon was the head of housekeeping in the mayor's mansion. In that role, Paula was responsible for seeing to it that the weekly rations of blood were either passed out or delivered to all the Loved Ones. Just as on any other ration day, Paula did just that.

But this would not be like any other ration day that the Loved Ones in Mayor Stout's sector would remember in the recent past.

Three trucks took off to deliver the rations that were due outside of the household around town. Paula saw to it that those inside got their weekly shares. It was then that she went into her own quarters to take her daily nourishment.

But, just as everyone else that fateful day, when she sat down to indulge, she was unable to stop. Just as Mason Stout had done in the early hours of the morning, she began to feast, and she lost all control, draining the bag completely. As a matter of fact, every last Loved One found themselves doing the exact same thing.

By five o'clock in the afternoon, all of them had gone into hiding and withdrawn into the darkness. They hid in pain from the sunlight and the sounds of the bustling city. They trembled and shook and shivered with what felt like sickness to their now unfamiliar bodies. They cried and screamed silent screams of anger and betrayal in the confines of their tortured minds.

Yes, it certainly seemed that the Dark Father had forsaken them all.

But Paula Harmon, even in her state, knew that something was very wrong. She wanted to speak with Mayor Stout, and she wanted to do it as soon as possible. She tried to leave her quarters on several occasions, only to run back into its loving arms after each feeble attempt. She knew what she had to do: when the darkness came, as soon as it came, she had to find him, and she had to do it right away.

But little did she know that, by the time the darkness came, any and all thoughts of seeking aid would disappear from her mind. She had no idea that as soon as the sun safely set she would be doing what everyone else in her sector would be doing.

Taking to the skies and hunting…

∞

It was exactly seven twenty-eight in the evening, and Mike Biela, who had rented a motel room in a shabby dive out on a Philadelphia highway, was preparing to leave and head to Pittsburgh. There were two donation centers he had tracked down that he wanted to thoroughly case out. It was important to be ahead of the game for Mayor Stout and next week's haul.

He stepped out of the shower and wiped the steam off the mirror with a hand towel, then set about drying his hair and body with a larger one. Mike hummed as he did this; he was feeling on top of the world. Things were finally looking up, and life was beginning to go his way, it seemed.

He stepped out of the bathroom, naked, and put deodorant on, then proceeded to put on a pair of new black jeans and a black hooded sweatshirt. He combed his hair, then popped open a small package of jalapeno potato chips and put two into his mouth. He loved those things.

Mike snatched his cigarettes and lighter off the nightstand by the bed, then grabbed his room key and tucked it safely into his front jeans pocket. Next, he turned the television on and flipped through the channels of the old tube-style television looking for the news. At least the place had basic cable, even if they didn't have porn. He needed to see the weather, and he wasn't quite ready to leave until he did just that. Call it a minor addiction, watching the weather if he was able; he didn't care. At least he tried to prepare for things properly.

Someone knocked on the door.

Mike hit the mute button on the television remote and listened carefully, sitting still on the foot of the bed. Was that a knock? Who would be knocking on his door? The only possibility he could think of was the cops. He glanced at the clock as he listened: ten minutes to eight. The knock came again, lighter this time, but yes, it was there.

"Who is it?"

Mike listened closely but received no response. He stared blankly, his heart pounding. It would definitely not be the cops, he thought. The cops would have answered, and answered loudly. Was it the manager? Or maybe someone had the wrong room.

"Hello?"

When he didn't receive an answer that time, he simply stood up and walked over to the large double window. He moved aside one of the heavy lined curtains, but only slightly, just enough to see the parking lot and the area just outside his door: both appeared barren and still. There wasn't even another car, besides his van, in the parking lot, just as it had been when he arrived at the motel. Even the manager had said he was the only guest at the time.

Mike shrugged and let the curtain fall back into place, then started for the bed. Suddenly there was another knock, but this one was much harder and more persistent. He nearly jumped out of his skin, and that fact pissed Mike Biela off. He turned sharply to the door and turned the knob.

"I said, who is…"

He was hit with what felt like a ton of bricks, or a semi. The impact picked Mike up off his feet and carried him across the room, smashing him into the far wall. Someone, or something, was on him.

He began to struggle in earnest against the weight that was on top of him. But, like in a dream, he felt as though he had no strength. His arms and legs felt heavy and powerless, but he continued to try to fight. He also tried to see, but whatever it was seemed to be a blur over him.

As if on cue, the thing stopped moving and looked down at him; Mike looked up at the exact same time.

It was Mayor Mason Stout. He had hold of Mike's arms and straddled the rest of him in a way so full of power and strength that it rendered the man completely motionless, except for the terribly rapid rise and fall of his chest as he panted with both fear and exhaustion. Stout smiled down at him, and a long string of saliva fell from his lips and hit Mike right in the middle of the forehead.

"Hello, Michael."

Mike's face softened slightly with recognition. He then noticed the redness of the man's eyes, and it made his blood run cold. "Mr. Stout, I–"

But he never finished his sentence. With a swoop so fast it was almost undetectable with the human eye, Stout bent and took Mike's neck in his mouth, sinking his razor-sharp teeth directly into the man's jugular as though he were tapping a keg of beer. Mike Biela's eyes went wide, and he tried to scream, but no sound went out. He could feel the blood leaving his body, feel each and every suck, and he could even feel Stout gulping after each one.

His vision started to blur, and he was aware that he

was cold, so cold. His mind could not wrap around what was happening to him. Mike seemed to think, for some reason, that his new boss was giving him a hug of appreciation for a job well done. His mind ceased to make any sense for a bit, then it fizzled out altogether as he died.

Stout sat up and dragged the sleeve of his long black robe over his mouth, smearing blood across his cheek as he did so, even getting some in his hair. His eyes were closed, and his breathing was labored. His ears were ringing pleasingly, and he found himself caught up in the sound.

After five full minutes, his breathing had calmed, and he opened his eyes. The first thing he did was look around the room, and when he did so there was an obvious question in his eyes. The door was hanging open, and he could see the full expanse of star-spangled sky. It was then that he actually looked down, and an alarm seemed to go off in his head when he realized that the pale, drained body beneath him was actually that of his new provider, Mike Biela.

Now it was coming back to him: the sun going down and him thieving into the night. He couldn't remember anything but the scent. It had pulled him directly to it, and he had paid no mindfulness to who it might lead to. He had been simply instinctual at that point, and he'd obeyed its voice fully.

He felt no remorse of any kind. He had fed, so it wasn't like he had to worry about next week's hook-up, and he was certain his regression into what he used to be was not going to go away any time soon. No, he was pretty sure it was here to stay.

The only thing he feared was what his consequences were to be when Ira Stone found out, and the Dark Father was sure to lead him to the truth.

Yes, there were going to be consequences to pay.

Of that, Mason Stout was positive.

R.W.K. Clark

# CHAPTER 12

The truth was that Mason Stout needn't have worried at all. His little indiscretion would be the least of the worries for the entirety of the Family of the Dark Order. All over Philadelphia, disorder was breaking loose.

The sun had no sooner set the same evening, then each and every vampire in the mayor's sector whisked away in the night, taking to the sky or moving like lightning on foot. Each was led by a very individual scent of fresh blood, and each pursued it with success until its source was found and devoured. Over 70 of the living were slain, their bodies ravaged and left to rot. None were bitten for the change, for not one of the Loved Ones had the self-control to stop feasting.

By the time the sun came up on the horizon the following morning, televisions and radios across the nation were mad with the chaos of the mass deaths in Philadelphia. The public was hysterical, and the government was beside itself. No one could find Mayor Stout, however. It was assumed he was one of the dead, and his body would be found like all the others. But the truth was a much more jagged pill to swallow.

In reality, Stout's sector and all of the Loved Ones in it had gone into hiding. While Philadelphia lost its mind in those early morning hours, its mayor and his minions slept peacefully in a deep, hidden cavern in the heart of Benjamin Rush State Park. It didn't take long for Ira Stone, who was having his dawn coffee, to find out that he had his hands very, very full.

He was listening to the morning news, which he had tuned into via the television in his kitchen. He had a long day ahead in a marathon board meeting for his company, Stone & Kimble Pharmaceuticals. They were involved with a genetics company called GenetiLabs, which was working on a revolutionary cancer treatment for the blood, and Stone and Kimble would be their producers. He had gotten a call the day prior telling him that GenetiLabs had been robbed, but he didn't expect to find out what had been taken specifically until the meeting that day.

But then, as he sipped his steaming java, the announcement of the murders in Philadelphia came blaring from the television. An icy finger traced Stone's spine, and he dropped the coffee cup to the ground, shattering it. He could not believe what he was hearing.

Bodies, thirty-seven at that time and still counting, were turning up all over the city and its outskirts. It wasn't just the killings that disturbed Ira; it was the manner in which each and every victim had been slain. The bodies had been completely drained of blood by means of a double puncture mark on the neck. No other damage or mutilation had been done.

His first reaction was to grab his cell and speed-dial Mason Stout.

The phone rang and rang endlessly. Ira wanted to scream into the device and will Stout to answer, but he already knew deep in his mind that Stout wasn't about to answer. The sector leader had somehow succumbed, and so had all in his charge. Ira Stone would be the one to have to deal with the Dark Father.

The thought made him cringe, but now was certainly not the time to scurry with fear. He needed information, and he needed it fast. What had the power to supersede the gift the Dark Father had bestowed upon them, the gift of living and working among the living?

He had no idea, but something did.

He discarded his cell into a recliner as he made his way to his dressing room. There was no time to waste; he needed to confer with his assistant, Thorne Braun. Thorne had a special gift: he could discern the will of the Dark Father. But Thorne did not have leadership skills or devotion to death. Ira Stone had both, so the Dark Father had placed the boy in the assistant position, so that Stone might receive the guidance he needed to properly lead the Loved Ones.

He dressed at the speed of light and rushed back to his cell. Ira punched in Thorne's cellular number while he put his jacket on. The phone rang while Stone went back to his room for his wallet.

"Yes, sir?" Thorne answered.

Ira's eyes closed with relief. "We have a terrible issue in Philadelphia, I'm afraid."

"Yes," Thorne replied. "I agree."

"I need you to confer with the Dark Father," Ira continued. "I am going to drive to your house in the meantime. We are going to Philadelphia. We have to track down Mason, and I cannot sense his location for some reason. We have to hurry."

"I'll see you soon, sir."

Usually Ira Stone used a driver, but he was in far too much of a rush to summon him. He had a sports car in his underground garage, and that would be the vehicle he would use today. As he hurried to it, he called his secretary at home to let her know he would be a little late for the meeting. He would call as soon as he was on his way. Until then, she would sit in his chair and take dictation of all minutes to that point. This issue with the robbery with GenetiLabs was simply too important to blow off altogether.

He started his car with a roar, revving it while waiting for the door to the tunnel drive to open. The worst thoughts were running through his mind; if this, indeed, was an explosion of defiance from Stout's sector, the Dark Father might wipe them all out with a wave of his hand. For one of the undead, Ira Stone was experiencing fear in a way he hadn't in centuries.

∞

By ten thirty that morning, Ira Stone and Thorne Braun had swept a few nearby homes and workplaces of Loved Ones, and not a single one could be found.

On the way to Stone's office to join the meeting, the dread and apprehension he felt filled the air in his tiny car. He sat in silence, knowing that Thorne was constantly tuned into the Dark Father and that he would speak of their next step as soon as it had been divulged to him. He thought the time would never come.

But soon, the time did come.

"This is not the fault of Mason Stone," Thorne said suddenly and simply.

Ira looked over at him as they sat at the red light. "What do you mean?"

Thorne squinted as if he were trying to see something blurry in the distance. "The Dark Father," he said. "He is impressing upon me that something or someone interfered with the gift, something usurped its power."

Stone didn't even try to converse with the man while driving. He passed through the light once it turned green, then pulled his sports car into the parking lot of a bustling supermarket. When he had parked it, he turned to Thorne with full attention and expectation.

"Something about the blood," he continued.

Ira was trying to sort out the vague information and relate it to the reality they all lived. The back alley blood deals and the shady connections. Mason Stout had been having problems with his provider; could something have driven them to this? Had they run out of sustenance?

Now Thorne tied it off with a bow. "The blood… the blood was bad. It was tainted, not pure. It was for the sick, but it wasn't ready."

GenetiLabs! Their robbery! It was like it became clear, and he knew that somehow the two situations were tied together.

"What am I to do, Thorne?" he asked his assistant. "What does the Dark Father require?"

Thorne Braun did not respond right away. He continued to squint, his eyes darting here and there at the activity going on outside the car. It was as if he were listening to a voice that no one but he could hear.

It seemed that hours were passing to Ira as he waited for direction. Composure was essential, however, and he held himself firmly, not allowing himself to indulge in nervous jitters or finger-tapping. The Dark Father would not be pleased with antsiness, which caused inevitable interruption to the unheard conversation Thorne was having.

Finally, young Thorne spoke. "The Loved Ones are your responsibility. The renegades must be brought to the Dark Father for cleansing and a fresh giving of the old gift. But they will not come on their own in the state they are in. They are in a state of full defiance, and it is happening in their undead bodies; they have no say over themselves.

"Therefore you must bring them to him yourself, and you must start with the sector leader, Stout," Thorne continued. "He must be cleansed first. But you are going to have terrible trouble. They are strong, and he is the strongest. Their defiant attitudes and acts, the core of the sickness, edifies them horribly."

Ira turned and stared out the windshield, his mind

working a thousand miles an hour. What the Dark Father was trying to say was that he would have to be very ready, or he would be losing the fight to come in a very big way. He would be dragged into the sickness himself, and since he was the leader, there was no one else who would be able to bring him in for cleansing.

So, Ira Stone did exactly what a leader does. He bucked himself up and began to consider his options and what resources he had at his disposal. First, he would go to the meeting and find out all the details. Next, he would find Mason Stout and drag him to face the Father, which was exactly where he belonged.

# CHAPTER 13

Mason Stout's eyes opened, alert and wide awake.

It was pitch black in the cave, but he could see as clearly as if there were daylight shining all around. As a matter of fact, he couldn't remember ever seeing so clearly before. Everything was superbly sharp and clear, and it made his spine tingle with pleasure.

He could see all of those whom he had brought here with him, all the other Loved Ones who had been in his sector. They were all still sleeping; it seemed he was the only one who had smelled the sun going down. Somehow he knew by instinct that he had a sense they had not yet come into; the sun was not all the way down, and he knew it. As their leader, for some odd reason, he had awakened first, to prepare the night for their arrival.

He then realized that he could hear the breathing of the Loved Ones, and it was as loud as crashing in his ears. The sound caused a smile to curve across his lips. Yes, something was different; he hadn't felt so strong, powerful, and alive since he had been bitten himself, two centuries ago.

His mind told him this was a new, more refined

form of the Father's gift.

He convinced himself that the Dark Father was so pleased with him that he had lifted Mason Stout up over all other Loved Ones. He talked himself into believing that the Father wanted him to start the New Earth, wanted him and him alone to expand on the Family, making bigger and stronger Loved Ones to usher in the future.

Yes, Mason Stout had been chosen.

He swooped down from his roost on a shelf higher up in the cave, one overlooking the others so he could supervise and direct. They would be waking soon; the sun was continually creeping in its effort to hide from the beautiful moon. He began to pace as he waited impatiently. He wanted to leave right away, for a scent had begun to beckon him, but he could not. He must wait until the others awoke, for their own lures would begin to draw them soon.

He would feast, and then he would begin his newly perceived work. He would begin to initiate the change in the living. He would begin to grow the vast family that he thought the Dark Father wanted, and he would work tirelessly at the task until the sun rose once again. He would do this every waking night until the desire and drive left him. The thought of bestowing his great power and lust into others made him feel omnipotent.

This is what being a vampire is all about. Not working lowly, menial jobs and serving the living. Not wearing fine clothing or driving fancy cars just for show. Most certainly not sucking the blood out of a plastic bag! No, it was about the hunt, and about the process of sharing eternity with those who didn't even believe it could exist, those who sought salvation in churches, the living.

The others began to stir, and it made his heart swell with purpose. He stopped panting, and as their eyes fluttered open and they rose in his presence, he spread his arms out before them. When the last one had been fully stirred, Mason Stout spoke.

"Go!" He hollered at the top of his lungs. "Feast and enjoy the blackness and security of the night and the moon. I will see you when the sun begins to rise, and we will rest together, full of our indulgence and satisfaction. Be free!"

With a sound much like that of horrific thunder, Mason Stout and his new family of Loved Ones took to the night.

∞

"Welcome to KRNP, Philadelphia's Most Dependable and Thorough Morning News," the television blared. "This is Vaughn Jennings with your morning news.

"Countless residents of the city have reported sightings of the Philly Mass Murderers, the unknown assailants who left a body count the night before last that is still rising as I speak." The sandy-haired man on the television was trying to take on a serious expression, but he was failing miserably. An Oscar-winning actor he would never be. "Over the course of the night several calls were received by both police and television news channels claiming to have witnessed vampires, that's right, vampires, chasing and literally attacking and biting many citizens. At every sighting, a new victim's body was found, and there were even reports of a handful of people who were bitten, but not drained or killed. Here is Megan Joy with an on-location report."

The screen flipped to show a plastic-looking blonde with bushy eyebrows and fuchsia lipstick standing rigidly in front of Sister Cities Park. She wore a nervous, frightened look and kept glancing back and forth as though she were looking out for a mugger or something. "Thank you, Vaughn. It seems the terror in Philadelphia has only just begun, and vampires are real. According to scores of witnesses, individuals have been seen, and even photographed by many, running through the night and attacking civilians. While many bodies are currently being discovered in the aftermath, there have also been reports by those who have been bitten but were not killed. The city, quite literally, is in a state of hysteria. People are calling in sick to work and locking themselves in their homes, which is exactly what has been recommended by law enforcement.

"Another point of major concern is the fact that neither our fair city's mayor, Mason Stout, nor any member of his staff have been found. Authorities are diligently searching for the mayor, but so far have had no luck." The woman nervously switched her microphone from one hand to the other. "Several others in the city have gone missing, though no family filed the reports. A variety of employers filed them, stating that they didn't show up for their scheduled shifts. Are the missing persons cases related to the murders in some way? Police reassure everyone that they will not stop until they find out. This is Megan Joy, live at Sister Cities Park. Back to you Vaughn."

Ira held up the remote control and muted the set before turning his eyes to Thorne. He had asked his assistant to seek guidance from the Father as to what he wanted him to do specifically to withstand Stout and his newfound strength; now it was just a matter of getting the word. Ira would fight to the death to rein in the plague and bring the people back into submission.

At the meeting, the day before he had learned that GenetiLabs had been robbed of gallons of genetically altered blood, and Ira was sure this was exactly what Stout had somehow gotten his hands on. Dr. Quentin Varney had explained, in great detail, how strong the blood was, why it wasn't ready, and what its effects were on the lab animals. Stout's guy must have stolen the blood, and now this was the result.

Suddenly the intercom on his desk went off. "Mr. Stone, Dr. Quentin Varney is here to see you."

"Send him in, Hillary."

Within only moments the door to his office opened, and Quentin Varney entered, accompanied by Allen Chandler of GenetiLabs. Ira and Thorne both stood, and the men shook hands all around. When they were finished, Ira gestured to the chairs opposite of his desk.

"Please, sit," he said. "I understand you have information regarding the rash of… vampire attacks."

The men sat, then Varney began. "Yes, Mr. Stone. I can tell you with certainty that this… vampirism… is a direct result of the ingestion of this blood."

Stone walked to his office window and began to stare outside. He watched the hustle and bustle in the main parking lot of Stone & Kimble without saying a thing. Obviously, the men weren't aware that all of the vampires were already just that. They were blaming the vampirism directly on the tainted blood, and that was something of a relief for Stone, the Dark Dominant of the Loved Ones the world over.

"Okay," he replied simply.

"Also, you may take comfort in the fact that even those who have been bitten by these people will not be affected in such a profound way," Varney continued. "In order for the person to turn so violent they would have to ingest the tainted blood for themselves, so we have that going for us."

Ira continued to listen in silence as the man droned on, but his mind was far from the words. It was, indeed, a relief to know that the newly bitten wouldn't be so strong; it would make it easier to bring them into the Dark Father's fold and in his will. But when it came to Mason Stout and those in his sector who had taken the bad blood, well, Ira Stone was at a complete loss.

After another twenty minutes of discussion, the two men from GenetiLabs left, leaving the promise of keeping Stone up to date on any new discoveries. The blood they still had was under both lock and key and heavy guard; there would be no second robbery. Of that they were certain, but that fact did very little to ease Ira's mind.

Immediately after the men left, Thorne said, "The Father has spoken as to what you are to do."

Ira gave him immediate attention. "And?"

"Nothing," Thorne said simply. "You are to do nothing. The Father will see to it that Stout's defiance, and that of the others, runs its proper course."

# CHAPTER 14

The days were turning into weeks.

Mason Stout sat in a hotel room, the heavy curtains were drawn to keep the sun out, and a 'Do Not Disturb' sign dangling from the knob on the outside of the door. He was both angry and ravenous, and it was a combination which was slowly driving him even madder than he had gone when he drank the blood Mike Biela had brought him. He had to figure things out, and he had to do it fast.

Stout had completely lost control, and though he knew it, he couldn't care less. He was at a definite crossroads. He had been feasting, and he had been working to initiate the change in select others, but nothing seemed to be working out as it should, as he had envisioned it would.

When he began the work he thought those upon whom he brought the change would be like him: incredibly strong, ultra-powerful senses, and unparalleled intelligence. But he had soon learned that the new breed had nothing in common with him, and he began to systematically seek them out and destroy them. As the head of the breed he had that power, but it had brought him little to no satisfaction.

With this unsettling feeling came something even worse: feasting on the normal living began having no effect. His appetite was insatiable for blood, but not just any blood. He wanted more of what Biela had brought him. Unfortunately, Biela had been his first victim, and he had no idea where the man had gotten the blood which had changed him so dramatically.

In the last week, in an effort to quench this horrible thirst, Mason began to kill his own. He began draining those in his sector, those who had been changed right along with him. He thought their blood might do the trick, and it did, but only for a short time before the hunger took over once again.

Now he was the only one left. He had managed to murder each and every Loved One who had been under his supervision, draining them and discarding their once immortal bodies like used rubbish. He had quite literally littered the city of Philadelphia with them, and he had no desire to reverse time and change things. But he had to get his hands on more of that special blood, and that was his only focus. So obsessed was he that it caused him physical pain.

Tonight, he would kill one, feast, and then he had determined to begin to search for some of the blood he so desired. He had no idea how he would accomplish that feat, but he intended to do so fully. For now, though, all he could do was toss and turn on the shabby hotel mattress and wait for the sun to go down.

Clint Murray hummed to himself as he left Stone & Kimble Pharmaceuticals. It was nearly eight in the evening, and he had put in a twelve-hour day as a driver for GenetiLabs, but he didn't mind. With another baby on the way, Clint needed all the overtime he could get.

He put the key into the GenetiLabs van door and unlocked it, hopping inside and making himself comfortable. He had just transported three bags of blood to Stone & Kimble, where Dr. Quentin Varney and some of the Stone & Kimble laboratory staff were going to pull an all-nighter studying it. He knew something big was going on because everyone was all business, not a smile in the place. He couldn't care less, though. He just wanted to get the van back to GenetiLabs and go home to his family.

As he steered the van along the interstate he sang along with a country and western song on the radio, oblivious to the fact that he was being tailed, but not by another car.

In the skies above the van, Mason Stout was flying. He had smelled just what he wanted: the new blood. It was coming from the van below him, though the scent was very weak indeed. No more than a lingering afterthought. He didn't believe that the blood was in the van, but he firmly believed that it had been not so long ago. The point was, wherever this van was either going to or coming from was where he was going to find what he was looking for.

So he flew, keeping the van in his sight and staying

exactly above it through every curve and turn. He would hover when it hit red lights or stop signs, and he would take flight again when it began to move. It didn't take long, just under a half-hour, and the van was pulling into a darkly lit business parking lot.

GenetiLabs.

Mason Stout perched himself atop a DeliverQuik drop box across the street and down about a half-block. He watched as the man in the van parked it and then got out of the vehicle to be met by another in a security guard uniform. The smell of the blood was so strong here that it made Mason's head spin so strongly it rivaled being drunk.

"Hey, Clint," the man in the security uniform greeted the driver. "I take it you are finally ready to head home? Everything went smoothly at Stone & Kimble, I take it?"

"Hey, Chuck. Yeah, it did," the driver replied. "And I can't wait to get home, but that's another half-hour drive. I'd stay and chat, but my wife's reheated meatloaf is calling my name loud and clear."

Chuck Hunter laughed like it was the funniest thing he had ever heard. Everyone at GenetiLabs knew that Clint Murray's wife couldn't cook worth a darn. "I'd say have a piece for me, but I have a feeling that my bologna sandwich is far better."

"And you're pretty much right," Clint added with a smile.

The driver then walked to one of the two cars still in the GenetiLabs lot, a small, beat-up sedan.

"Well, you have a good night then, Clint," Chuck said with a wave.

Clint waved back. "You do the same, and be safe doing it, ya hear?"

With that he climbed into his rat-trap car and drove out of the lot, his taillights disappearing as he steered himself away from the disaster that was about to happen.

When Mason saw the taillights disappear around the corner, he took immediate flight. The guard, Chuck, was walking back into the building through a side door, but he never made it. Stout came down on him with the force of a truck, slamming him to the floor and sinking his teeth into the man's neck. It wasn't this man's blood he was after, but since he had to die anyway, why not make a meal out of him? In less than two minutes his body was completely drained, and it lay lifeless, eyes wide open, on the floor.

"Well, so much for your bologna sandwich, Chuck," Stout said.

He turned on his heel and let the door slam shut behind him, Chuck Hunter the security guard forgotten. Now Stout was being led by the smell of that blood, the blood that would be in a refrigerator. It took him less than thirty seconds to find it.

With a quick jerk of the handle, he flung the door open, and an alarm began to blare obnoxiously, complete with flashing lights. The police would be on their way, not that he cared. He would be long gone by the time they arrived.

He loaded his arms up with bags, and seconds later Mason Stout took back to the Philadelphia nighttime skies. He flew like lightning, his arms filled with bags, and soon he was at the window of his hotel room, which he had left open when he flew off that evening. He flew inside, dropped the bags on the bed, and closed the window and blinds.

Now he could feast, and feast he did.

Mason drained an entire bag in no time, and he suddenly felt the rush of added power he had been seeking for so long. It was deafening and invigorating. It made him want to scream with relief, but instead, he just sat on the floor next to the bed. His eyes closed and the sound of his own blood pumping filling his ears, sounding much like the beloved siren he loved so much. He sat like that, in his orgasmic state, for what seemed like an eternity but was actually only minutes.

Now he felt better.

He finally stood up and picked up all the bags remaining in the middle of the bed. He was thankful at that minute for the small refrigerator that came with his room, and as he put the bags inside of it, he whistled cheerfully.

He had found what he had been looking for, and he was smugly satisfied.

# CHAPTER 15

The ringing of the telephone rudely ripped into Sasha Hunter's dreams, tearing her from their embrace and making her angry. She first realized it was daylight, then squinted at the clock on her nightstand. It was nearly eight in the morning. Another day off of school and she had been robbed of sleeping in.

Sasha picked up the phone and uttered a groggy, "Hello…"

"Sasha, it's Aunt Sadie," the woman's voice said. "Did I just wake you?"

Even in her dazed state of consciousness, Sasha heard something in her aunt's voice, something off. "Yes, but that's okay. What's going on, Sadie?"

The woman paused on the line for a moment, then said, "I take it the police haven't contacted you?"

"Police?" Now Sadie had Sasha's full attention, and she swung her legs over the side of the bed to bring herself to a higher state of being alert. "Why would the police get a hold of me? What's wrong?"

Another pause, then when Sadie spoke her voice cracked with emotion. "I guess that's because I was his only emergency contact."

Sasha became horribly confused. "Aunt Sadie, what are you talking about?"

"Chuck," Sadie replied. "Your father, Sasha. He was... he was killed at work last night."

"What the heck are you talking about?"

"The alarm went off," the woman continued. "And when the police responded they, found him."

"What do you mean, 'they found him'?"

"Your father has been murdered," she concluded. "His blood was drained. They say they suspect it was one of those forsaken vampire attacks. I'm so sorry, Sasha."

Now Sadie broke fully into tears on the other end of the phone, but Sasha didn't hear it. She dropped the receiver on the floor as shock coursed through her body. She then jumped up and ran to her father's room. The door was closed, just as it always was in the morning, since he worked the night shift and needed sleep. Of course he wasn't dead; he was just in his room, asleep. They had obviously made a mistake.

Sasha knocked on the door. "Daddy?"

There was no answer, so she knocked harder. "Daddy, wake up, I need to talk to you."

By now her heart was pounding, and it was telling her the truth about what her head didn't want to admit. She grabbed the knob, turned it, and shoved the door open. Sun from the open window flowed through the window and lit the perfectly made bed as though it were shoving its neatness in her face.

"No," Sasha screamed, then the tears choked her.

She stumbled into the room and looked at the bed in disbelief, but only for a moment. Then she ran from the room and began to rush around the house.

"Daddy?!"

But all of her cries came back to her, empty and barren. Her father wasn't home, and that was a painful fact. Right then a sharp rapping came at the front door of the small bungalow she shared with her father.

"Miss Hunter, are you home?" It was a man's voice, and it sounded very official. "It's Detective McAllister of the Philadelphia police. I need to speak with you, Miss Hunter."

Sasha simply stood and stared at the door, tears running down her cheeks. It was true. She couldn't deny it. Now it was time for her to buck up and open that door. She would do so with great hope that there had been some kind of mistake.

With a turn of the knob and a quick jerk, Sasha opened the front door. It took all of her strength to speak to the man in the suit and tie on her step and the uniformed officer with him. Her lower lip trembled.

"How can I help you, Detective?"

The man couldn't look her in the eye. His hands were in the pockets of the jacket he was wearing. He looked at the ground, then back at the attractive young lady who had obviously been crying. She must have found out from the aunt.

"I take it you have been informed?" he asked.

Sasha wiped at her eyes with the backs of her hands. "Please, come in. I need to know what happened."

She held the door open for them, and the two men entered the small living room. "Please, have a seat."

She plucked a tissue from a box on an end table and sat in her father's recliner. "How did it happen?"

"First of all, I'm so sorry that this has happened to you," Detective McAllister said. "I can't begin to imagine how you must be feeling. With that being said, an alarm was tripped at GenetiLabs. Police responded immediately due to their recent robbery and what has been released by them regarding the stolen blood and the rash of vampire murders. They reached the place in record time. Your father was found just outside the doorway of the building. He was already gone when they arrived. I'm sorry, once again."

Sasha nodded and blew her nose. "My aunt, Sadie Roarke, just called and told me."

"Yes, she was his emergency contact," he replied. "But she is out of town, as you well know. She did give us your information. I'm going to need you to identify his body, Miss Hunter."

Sasha didn't answer him right away. Her mind was racing, and nothing that came to it made any sense at all. She had just spoken with him on the phone the prior evening. He sounded so cheerful. Her heart was broken in her chest; Sasha was closer to no one on the planet than her father. What was she going to do?

"Miss Hunter." McAllister's voice interjected in her thoughts. "Did you hear me?"

Now she nodded. "I'll just need to put some clothes on. Do you want me to meet you?"

"No, ma'am," he said gently. "You shouldn't be driving. We'll take you and bring you home when we're finished."

"Of course," she told him. "I'll just be a minute."

Fifteen minutes later they were on the road and in route to the morgue. Sasha had stopped crying, but she was still numb with disbelief. How had this happened? She wanted to know who had done this, who had stolen her only close family member from her so suddenly and violently.

The identification went quickly, and to Sasha Hunter, it was a blurry nightmare. Yes, indeed. It had been her father lying on that slab, completely ashen and lifeless. She did what she had to do and left the room in a thunderous rush of emotion that threatened to steal her consciousness. Until she was on her way home, in the back of the police cruiser, she was beside herself because of the identification process.

"Do you people have any suspects?" she asked absently as they drove.

Detective McAllister, who was seated in the front passenger seat, turned to her. "Yes, Miss Hunter. We do. As a matter of fact, we are fairly positive we know who has been doing all of the killing. The issue isn't our lack of knowledge. The issue is that the suspect, at least up until now, has evaded capture."

They knew? "Does the public know?"

"Yes, it has been on the news," McAllister replied. "I take it you don't watch much television."

She shook her head absently. "I attend the

university; I hardly have time to breathe. I am also a very busy sculptress, and I also spend time teaching self-defense to children, when my schedule allows it."

"I see," he said. "Camera footage from both security cameras around the city and photos and videos taken of murders by citizens with cell phones have shown us that the guilty party is, unfortunately, Mayor Mason Stout."

Sasha's head turned sharply toward the detective. "The mayor? You are trying to tell me the mayor of this city is responsible for the killings?"

"It appears that way," he replied softly. "However, when we do catch him, he will have to face a jury of his peers, but he's very slippery. Very slippery indeed."

The car pulled into her driveway, but Sasha didn't realize it. Her mind was on Mason Stout, the man who, according to cameras, had killed her father. She was enraged, so much so that she didn't even know what was going on around her.

"Miss Hunter, here we are."

The sound of McAllister's voice snapped her out of her reverie. "Thank you, gentlemen," she said as he hopped out and opened the rear door for her. She alit from the vehicle and turned to McAllister. "I certainly hope you people become as slippery as he."

"Are you going to be all right alone?" he asked.

She nodded at him and offered him a weak smile. "Yes, I'll be fine. Thank you both."

With that, Sasha Hunter turned her back to the officers and walked to her house. Once she was safe inside, she sat in her father's recliner once again, and she let herself cry until the tears would come no more. But it was only the tears that ceased; the rage stayed, and it grew larger and more powerful inside of her.

The police couldn't catch him. Slippery... that was what McAllister had called Mason Stout. Slippery. What a joke. If they couldn't get him there was a reason, and she leaned toward the simplest explanation: the man was truly a vampire.

It was time to learn a bit about Mason Stout.

∞

Mason was doing much better since he had acquired the blood his body so craved.

It was noon, and he was once again holed up in his room, watching the television news, which was focused almost completely on him and his recent antics. He was relieved he had disguised himself and used the identification of one of his victims to secure the hotel room. He had checked in under the name 'Kevin Stanley.' If he hadn't handled things that way, they certainly would have tracked him down and apprehended him by now. He chalked it up to his keen intelligence and thanked Satan under his breath for the gift of it.

Yes, dismay had seemingly broken loose in Philly, and every last shred of that disturbance could be attributed to him. It made him feel good to know he had authored such an outstanding level of chaos, but he was only just getting started. He had so much to look forward to since finding the blood and the place it was kept. Now he didn't have to venture out into the night to kill for his meals, but he chose to kill anyway. After all, it was the nature of the beast that he was. He felt no remorse; as a matter of fact, he was entertained by the fear and hysteria he had bred.

When the sun went down tonight, he intended to actually fly all the way to Pittsburgh. Who knew what kind of tasty morsels he would encounter there? Yes, it was time to indulge in the buffet of the living that the Dark Father had laid out before him so generously.

Pittsburgh it was…

∞

"Excuse me. Do I need a password for your Wi-Fi?"

Sasha Hunter stood at the main desk of the Philadelphia Public Library. Usually, she used the Wi-Fi at school when researching, but she hadn't gone in the last few days, not since finding out about her father. Her priorities had been forever changed that day.

"No, ma'am," the librarian said. "Just hook up to the open, unsecured signal. You should be good to go!"

The woman offered Sasha a bright smile, and Sasha gave her one back, though it was forced and fake through and through. She left the woman, laptop in tow, and began to look around for a private area in which to begin her research on the beloved mayor of her fair city.

Soon she was seated, laptop open and online. The contents of her bag were spread out on the desk as well. Notebook, pencils, and sharpener. She would definitely be taking notes during this little study session.

She had also begun watching the news pretty much

all day long. It was essential that she do so now. Especially since she fully intended to hunt that bloodsucking so-and-so down herself. She needed to keep track of any murders he committed if she was going to find him. Last night he had actually ventured to Pittsburgh, and the people there were coming all unglued.

Now, as she began her research, all of that was put out of her mind in exchange for all things Mason Stout.

It began as basically as it could, from the 'beginning' of his life. It seemed that Stout had been orphaned, or at least, that was what the public records told her. It seemed his family, who were very prominent in the area, owned a mill, or so he had said. It had burned down, leaving poor little Mason all alone in the world.

The first photo on record of the man was taken when he was the head of a company called Stout Enterprises. It was a computer firm that seemed to have its hand in all sorts of digital aspirations. She recalled having heard of it, but Sasha had always been a bit more artsy than technically inclined. She did know that the business was very profitable, and according to what she was learning, Stout didn't even need his mayor's salary to live a comfortable life.

He began to dabble in politics five-and-a-half years ago when he won his first mayoral election. He had just been elected for his second term last fall. Photos became very common by the time she reached that point.

She noted that, according to Stout, he had been

born in the small town of Genesee Township. So Sasha decided to try to find any history on his family that she could. But Sasha Hunter was in for a big surprise.

Yes, there had been a 'Stout' family in the area right around the time the thirty-nine-year-old mayor had been born. Yes, they had owned a textile mill, and yes, it had burned to the ground, killing both his mother and father, as well as more than seventy of their employees. But that was as far as the truth went.

News articles said they did have a boy named Mason, but he had been killed in the fire right along with them.

Now her heart began to pound. If the mayor wasn't the real Mason Stout, who was he? She intended to find out.

But this would prove to be easier said than done. After another hour, she was at her wits' end, so she dug a sandwich out of her bag and took a break. When she was finished, she got her second wind and continued.

Sasha decided, at that point, to look into his father's background. It was a whim, nothing more, but it turned out to be the best decision she could have made. She was about to discover much more than she'd bargained for.

The man's name had been Tiberius Stout, and she found much information on the man. His being the head of a large company made him the topic of many news articles in the area at that time. He was known as the richest man in the area, so it was no surprise.

She began to read the articles. So many of them had

been written about the man. There were also records of a couple of television news interviews, but for now, she would stick with the things in print.

The first one did nothing but talk about Stout Textiles and a couple of donations Tiberius had made to the state hospital. The second talked about his wife and him expecting their first, and obviously only, child. The third actually had a photo of the infant and discussed his birth.

He was called Mason Joseph and, according to Tiberius, he was named after Mason Joseph Stout Tiberius' great-great-grandfather. He had been much loved by all, but unfortunately, this Mason had been murdered, or so it was thought. He disappeared after a home invasion that left his wife dead. The only survivor had been a single son, James Watson Stout, Tiberius' great-grandfather.

What Sasha saw next took her breath away.

There were actually two photographs accompanying the article, which had been published in a newspaper from another small town near Genesee. The entire article was split over two pages. The first half was on the front page, along with the photo of Mr. and Mrs. Stout and baby Mason.

But there, at the bottom of the first half, in tiny letters, it said, 'cont. on page 4A'. There was obviously more to read. So Sasha entered the proper commands and soon, on 4A, she saw, 'Tiberius Stout, continued.'

She began to read, but her eyes were drawn to another photo, this one accompanying the second half of the article. In the photo, Tiberius Stout was holding a dreadfully old photo. It had been framed with wood, and Stout was smiling with pride as he held it and shared it with the public. The caption beneath read:

Mason Joseph Stout, great-great-grandfather of Tiberius, circa 1810

The photo was either of a striking look-alike of the mayor, or it was of the mayor himself; he was identical in all ways, except for the style of clothing he wore.

Sasha sat back hard in her chair. She was staring straight ahead, and she was holding her breath, though she didn't realize it. Regardless, her mind knew with a solid surety that the authorities in Philly had no clue Mayor Mason Stout was, indeed, a vampire.

Not one who had been made by drinking tainted blood, as the news and public supposed, dragging him into the role of victim with their suppositions. No, he had been a vampire for a very long time. From the looks of it, he had been one since his untimely disappearance over two centuries ago.

Sasha decided that her next best step would be to find out what she could about vampires, so the search began. It didn't take her long to realize that much of what she read was supposed and made-up garbage. Storytellers and yarn-spinners had had their way with the topic for centuries, but what she did discover, and believed, was that they had to have blood.

Somehow, though, for years and years, the monsters had been living among people without killing. She discovered a fairly recent article which theorized that these particular undead had received a gift from Satan himself, their 'creator,' so to speak, which allowed them to live and work among the living. There were no specifics as to how they maintained themselves, but when she considered the robbery at GenetiLabs, she thought she had a pretty solid idea.

Everything made sense then. While she had no proof, she knew in her heart that the initial theft of blood from GenetiLabs had been conducted to provide the vampires with blood. Stout had likely been taking care of his urges like that for a very long time; it would have helped him stop killing. But the tainted blood had put him back into the murderous state he had once known, and now there was likely no going back.

But how could a vampire be stopped? Could one even really be killed or eliminated? Sasha Hunter decided, right then and there, that if the deed could be done, she was going to find out the truth about how. Not some shady, made-up story about eliminating them, but the real truth.

Then she was going to track the monster down and take care of him herself.

∞

Mason Stout had taken to sleeping during the daylight hours once again, finally, after so much time.

He lay in the darkness of his room, the heavy bedspread covering his entire body. He was in a deep state of rest; a bomb could have gone off right next to him, and it would not have roused him from his undead sleep in the slightest. But there was one thing that was tormenting him, even in his state: his dreams.

∞

The fog settled in around him; it was late at night, very late. Mason was seated on a stone bench, and, though he didn't know who he was waiting for, he knew he was waiting for someone. So wait he would.

But something was wrong. He was catching movements out of the corners of his eyes, first to the left, then to the right, then back again. His head jerked to and fro, and the icy fingers of true fear, an emotion he had not felt in two centuries, settled deep in the pit of his stomach.

Mason Stout was petrified.

His head jerked… there it was again!

"Who are you?" he screamed into the misty night. "Face me! Show yourself!"

Another shadow to the right, then to the left. His cold, dead hands began to tremble, and though he could see clearly in the darkness, he felt that something was truly hidden from his sight. What was happening?

It may be best to stand up and be on my guard, he thought to himself. He tried to stand, but his legs were weak, and his knees were knocking together. He stared down at them, horrified at their reluctance to cooperate. He felt like a weak baby.

"Ah, so you knew I would come for you, didn't you? You should have, you murdering idiot!"

Mason's head jerked up to see the dark figure of someone standing in the shadows about ten feet in front of him. He tried to see them clearly, but his eyes seemed as weak as his legs, and it made him want to cry in his frustration. He couldn't even tell if this was a man or woman speaking to him.

"Who are you?" he asked, trying to control the shaking in his voice and sound strong. "What do you want?"

"I want you to pay…"

Suddenly something rushed through the air past his head, and as it passed him by something sharp sliced into the skin of his cheek. Stout cried out, partially from panic and partially from pain. Had he felt that, really? His hand went up to his cheek and when he brought it to his face to look his hand was smeared with the blackness of his own blood.

"What do you want?"

He felt he might actually cry; he couldn't remember being so frightened, so vulnerable.

"I was loved by the one you have taken, and you do not scare me. Your turn to die!"

Another rush of wind and a deep slash across his back. This time he cried out loudly, arching his body as if to escape the stinging pain inflicted on him by the unseen. He fell off the bench and to his knees, his legs still incapable of following his instructions.

"That's right. Bow down. You are a worm of the evilest kind, and you deserve to die!"

Mason Stout began to sob. He closed his eyes and put his hands before his own face as if entering into prayer. His lips moved furiously, but no words came out for several seconds.

Finally he said, "Please, have mercy. It is by no fault of my own that I am what I am. Please!"

"A rabid dog isn't at fault, either, but we put them down for the good of all," the voice retorted. "You are a filthy, sick, rabid dog of the most perverse kind."

The voice was right in front of him. Stout opened his eyes, and there, only a foot before him was the same dark form. He couldn't make out any of the person's features, not its sex, its face, nothing. Tears fell freely, and he could barely catch his breath.

"P-P-Please, have mercy," he begged.

There was a soft chuckle. "Oh, I am."

With a single sweep of their arm, the person slashed at him, slicing his throat so deeply that his head was nearly taken off. Both his eyes and mouth flew open in disbelief, and the feeling of the pain was excruciating, but he was still alive. He watched with eyes set into a flopping head as the person's other arm swept back and forward. With a single strong, deft motion, a large wooden stake was driven right through his core…

∞

He woke with a start, sweat covering his cold body. His breathing was so ragged that he couldn't catch his breath. He wanted to cry out, but he wouldn't let himself; his hand quickly went to his mouth and covered it, his subconscious taking over to protect him.

What was that all about? He couldn't remember a dream like that since beginning his new life. He felt weak, exposed, and as if he were in terrible danger. Mason Stout was terribly shaken up.

Finally, he calmed a bit, and as he got his wits about him, he looked at the digital clock on the nightstand: six fifty-four in the evening. No point in resting anymore. The night would be upon him soon enough.

He felt enraged. Something was making him afraid, and that was something he was not accustomed to in the slightest. Fear had been taken from him when the change was first initiated. Why was he feeling it now?

As part of the gift of the living which the Dark Father had given them, they had the ability, through the Dark Dominant, Ira Stone, to approach the Dark Father and seek protection and guidance. But Mason was not about to go to Stone and ask for help. Something inside of him begged him to, but something in his mind refused to allow him to do it. What if they strung him up? What if the dream was telling him that they would murder him themselves for his crimes against the gift?

He sat up on the edge of the bed and put his head in his hands. It seemed that his mind was working a bit now, but only slightly, and it was fading fast. How had this happened to him? How had he fallen so far from the heights of the gift so quickly? He shook as he pondered it, but with each passing second the thoughts left him bit by bit, and they were replaced with thoughts of hitting the night skies on the hunt. Soon, the dream was no more than a mist of memory, and Mason could think about nothing but finding a fresh, warm drink. Not a cold one from the bags in the refrigerator, but one that would offer a scream of pain when he indulged. It took a living victim to do that.

Mason Stout was back to his animal self for yet another night.

# CHAPTER 16

Ira Stone parked his vehicle at a pull-off along a dirt road leading into the woods. Deep in the heart of those woods, there was a door, made of wood, and hidden in the midst of large rocks. It had been there for millennia, but it had never been found by the mortals. The Dark Father kept it safe.

The door led into the pit of the earth, and it was there that all of them, the Loved Ones, would meet. But this month the meeting was canceled or at least postponed. Thorne had told him that the Dark Father said he was to do nothing, but as the Dark Dominant, Ira felt the need to ask the Father to tell him that it would all be okay. Even if Mason was not to survive, Ira was deeply concerned for the rest of the Family.

Thorne would meet him here instead of just advising him. That would allow Ira to implore the Father on his own, and then the Father would communicate through Thorne immediately because they were in the 'Sacred Place.' It was as close to face-to-face as Ira Stone, or any of them would ever come to the Dark Father. Ira felt compelled.

He began his walk to the Sacred Place. Thorne was

already on his way to meet him there. Together they would venture into the deep. They would light the blood candles and pay homage to the Dark Father's greatness and generosity. Next, they would offer a living blood sacrifice, which would come from the small dove Ira was carrying in a small cage. Finally, he would approach the Dark Father with his concerns, and they would stay in the depths until he received an answer.

He reached the rocks and took a seat on the ground. Ira looked down at the small bird and said, "You have no idea what a privilege it is for you to die the death of your destiny, my fine feathered friend. It will be painless, and you will be honored for your sacrifice."

He clucked his tongue and whistled playfully at the animal several times, then stopped when he heard the rustling in the woods. Thorne had arrived. Ira's heart skipped an anxious beat; he wanted to get started. He wanted to beg for the Dark Father's mercy for those who remained under the gift.

Thorne appeared. "Greetings, Dark Dominant. You should know that the Dark Father approves of your decision to approach him on such a personal level over the dilemma our kind faces. He is eager to share his wisdom and will with you today."

Ira breathed a heavy sigh of relief. "Very good. It would never do to anger him after all he has done and continues to do for us, his children."

"No," Thorne replied. "He is not angry. He is impressed with your loyalty and desire to serve him properly. You are worthy of the position in which he has seated you, Dark Dominant."

Ira simply nodded and stood, grabbing the birdcage up as he did so. "Are you ready, Thorne?"

"I am more than ready."

Together the two men swooped upward and down between the rocks, where they opened the door in the ground and began their descent into the heart of the planet.

∞

Sasha Hunter spent the rest of the afternoon at the library. As a matter of fact, she was the last person to leave when they closed up for the day. The good news was that she had done a considerable amount of research, and she had learned more than she ever could have hoped for.

The first thing that she managed to bring to light was the fate of the young kid, the one the vampire Stout claimed to be. Obviously, it wasn't him; this Stout had lived for a couple of centuries. So, what had happened to the youngster born to the textile mill owner during the latter part of the seventies?

He was not seen or heard from again until his early thirties, when he revealed himself to the public in his bid for the mayor of Philadelphia and the president of Stout Enterprises. To Sasha, the truth was obvious: vampire Stout had stepped into his great-great-great grandson place in the world.

Sasha was narrowing things down quickly now, and a plan of action was quickly coming together in her head. Next, she would study the biggest question of all:

if vampires were indeed real, roaming the Earth and feeding, could they be killed? Or was killing vampires just a pipe dream thought up by the creative types in order to form a story where good always triumphs over evil? It was vital that she finds out.

So she began reading all she could get her hands on. From the looks of the materials she read, there was actually a long history of vampirism, and there was just as long a list of victims and heartbroken family members who were at a loss as to what could be done about the deaths of their family members. But vampires could, indeed, be taken out; 'killed' was not necessarily the correct term, but they could be eliminated from Earth and sent back to Purgatory from which they had been spawned.

Sasha discovered there were five legitimate ways to kill a vampire.

The first was by literally ripping its head off. This appeared to be the least popular of the methods, as the monsters healed so quickly. Silver, as in a blade, would slow down the healing process sufficiently for the job to be completed, but the issue was to get them to be still long enough for this to happen, and that wasn't likely. Another way to accomplish this was to actually either be another vampire, strong enough to actually rip the head from the body, or to be in cahoots with another one. She had neither of these in her favor, and, though she decided to take thorough notes, she put this particular method on the back burner.

Next was with sunlight. Sasha actually got a bit

excited about this method, as sunlight is abundant to the living. According to the literature, exposure to sunlight could completely destroy the vampire in only ten to fifteen seconds, but the trick was getting them to come into its rays. It would take a lot of maneuvering, intelligence, and manipulation to make this work out, and Sasha was a realist; this would probably not be her go-to solution. If it happened, it would be by accident.

Third, a vampire could be killed by use of fire. There was one serious issue with this option, however. Only sunlight and one other thing could successfully 'burn' a vampire, and they worked because they slowed down or stopped the healing process. While fire would burn them, they still healed at a high rate of speed. This meant the vampire would have to be trapped in a very, very hot fire for at least an hour to be consumed by it. Alone, she was not strong enough to accomplish the task, and she wasn't up for being institutionalized because she asked someone for assistance.

Which brought her to the fourth method, the other thing that would slow down or stop the healing: silver. The vampire's reaction to this metal was the result of silver's antibacterial properties. Silver would burn them and slow down their ability to heal, even stopping it altogether in some cases. According to the material, the use of silver was not quite as speedy or effective as sunlight or a wooden stake, but it would make a great weapon or tool to render them weak and sick, giving her the upper hand. The wonderful news was that Sasha was a sculptress, and she was extremely adept when it came to working with metal. This would definitely be information she could put to good use.

Finally, last but not least, the wooden stake. By all accounts, a stake through the heart of one of these monsters would kill them for good. But they were strong. It was recommended that the use of silver or sun weaken them. They would let their guard down, at which point putting the stake to good use would become easy.

Yes, she was forming a wonderful plan, and she was becoming very, very excited to exact her revenge.

Sasha bookmarked the things she found on her computer, packed her things up, and stood from her table just as the librarian announced that the library was closing. With a smile on her face she left, hearing nothing but the sound of the large double doors closing and locking behind her.

She had a lot of work to do, and it was time to get busy.

# CHAPTER 17

"He is too far gone, and he must be returned to the pit from which all of you came."

Thorne Braun was seated in the center of the pentagram, facing Ira Stone. His eyes were closed, and he appeared to be in something of a trance. To a human, it would be a very unsettling sight, but to a vampire, it was a thing of beauty to see and to hear the voice of the Dark Father.

Ira had gone before the Father after the dove's sacrifice and asked him what would become of Mason Stout. He wondered aloud how he might help, what he could do to contribute and save the rest of the Loved Ones from any curse Stout might have brought on all of them with his defiance. He expressed his willingness to obey any and all orders the Dark Father had for him.

One never knew how long they would have to wait for the Father's answer, so the two settled in and calmed themselves. Impatience would not be accepted. It was imperative that they remain calm, willing to wait out any storm the Father saw fit to put them through.

But they didn't have to wait long. As a matter of fact, less than five minutes had passed when Thorne's eyes closed tightly and his body tensed; the Dark Father had begun to fill him, speaking to his mind and preparing his tongue for his words. Stone watched in awe; what a gift it must be to have a direct line to the Father!

"How will he return to the pit, Dark Father?" Ira asked softly.

Thorne remained rigid, and his lips curved in a slight smile. "A girl. A human girl. His pride has taken control for a while. There is no better justice."

Ira knit his brow. "What girl would have this power, lord, and how can I help her?"

After a moment Thorne replied, "The daughter of one of the murdered. She has sufficient anger to accomplish the task, and I will strengthen her, for his return to me is my will. However, she will need you. Yes, she will."

Ira's eyes widened. What a blessing to rid the Loved Ones of Mason Stout's rotting presence, if that was what the Father required! "What can I do, Father? What would you have me do?"

Thorne twisted his head around as if listening to a distant, barely audible sound. "She will be busy preparing her tools. For now, simply watch her from afar. Observe how she does things, and if you believe she could use a bit of guidance, well, you will give it, but only without her seeing you... for now, anyway."

"But how?"

"Come to her in her sleep, if you must," Thorne continued. "You will meet face to face, but for now it cannot be. Her awareness of your presence will alert Stout to you, and he is far more powerful than you know."

Ira Stone considered all these words for a moment. Finally, he said, "I will do all you ask to the letter, Dark Father. Do I need her name?"

Thorne's head dropped, and he sat completely still. Would the Father not provide Ira with a name? Would he expect him to find her on his own? He would never be able to track her down in this city without more information.

Thorne's head snapped back up. "Sasha Hunter." His head dropped again, and his body went limp. The Dark Father had said all he was going to say.

The candles, which had been blazing during their conversation, now flickered back down into weak flame, and Ira felt the presence of the Dark Father leave the place. It left him with an empty, bittersweet feeling each and every time he left them, but this was their curse to carry—walk the Earth for eternity but be out of the presence of their creator.

It was Purgatory.

After a full ten minutes, Thorne raised his head, and his eyes fluttered open. He looked at Ira and smiled with satisfaction and even a look that said his hunger for the Father had been sated. His smile grew quickly when he saw the calm look on Ira's face.

"You have received good answers," he said. "You are satisfied."

Ira nodded. "Very satisfied. I will be busy. I will

need you to take care of things at Stone & Kimble, Thorne."

"I know," his assistant replied. "The Dark Father has already put it inside of me to do so. He will be sparing the remaining Loved Ones because of your obedience."

Ira nodded. He was very happy, and the peace which had eluded him for weeks was now back upon him. He rose from the floor, followed by Thorne. Time to re-enter the world of the living.

He had an angry little girl to track down.

∞

Sasha made a firm, yet frightening, decision: she would avenge her father's death, and she would become a warrior to get the job done. There was simply no other way. She couldn't confront this demon without that mindset and equal preparation. She was more than ready. She was ready to die trying if she had to.

For the first few days, Sasha busied herself with a task others would have laughed at considering the job at hand: she taught herself to work a lasso like a professional at a rodeo.

Why a lasso of all things? Her thought was this: if she was in the sun and he would not venture out, she would rope him and drag him, kicking and screaming, to his demise.

So, for the next three days, she focused only on working that rope. She practiced on part of a telephone pole her father had put in the ground in the backyard to mark off their fire pit. There were three of them, but she chose the tallest, just for the challenge.

She also began to work out vigorously and often. She had her father's weights, which he hadn't touched in years. She created a regimen, and she worked it like a woman obsessed. When she worked out in the darkened hours of dawn, she would push herself to the very limits of exhaustion, and she would purposefully recall all the self-defense moves she knew and taught to the children. She would practice kickboxing, something she had let herself go rusty on. With each passing day, she became stronger, more resilient, and faster than she had ever been in her life.

During the evening and earlier hours of the night, she worked with her silver.

College was now the furthest thing from her mind, and Sasha had dipped into her college money with a vengeance. She bought all the pure silver she could get her hands on, and she worked it in her small basement studio, the one her father had cordoned off just for her use. She had all the equipment needed to heat and work and form the metal, and she did it with great love. She created not only a beautiful sword engraved along the length of the blade with her father's name, but she also created terribly sharp blades which fit over the tips of her fingers and tightened comfortably there. She would wear them on her left hand so she could work her next creation easily with the strength of her right arm.

A crossbow, her father's favorite which he used for hunting. She used his arrows as a guideline for the slender wooden stakes she made, and she tipped each one with pure silver and carved his initials in each and every tip. She made sixty of these and fashioned something of a cartridge which held them all. It fitted beautifully on the crossbow, becoming a fluid part of the weapon. She loved the trigger mechanism which enabled her to shoot the stakes freely, one after the other, with astounding accuracy.

By the time Sasha Hunter was finished putting together her arsenal, most of her stress was gone. But the work did nothing for her bitterness and rage; as a matter of fact, it fed it. When she completed even the tiniest of steps, she would revel in her anger and allow it to motivate her. She would take it out on the weights and her other workout moves. The entire process took a month.

Ira Stone watched all that she did, approving greatly, and waited anxiously for Thorne to tell him when he could meet her face to face.

# CHAPTER 18

The murders in Philadelphia and Pittsburgh continued with dreadful regularity.

Each night, Mason Stout venture out into the darkness. Since scoring the tainted blood he had no need for the kill, but yet the kill beckoned him. He had to do it, had to follow the scent that called to him. Before the dream came to him, he had been satisfied with only one every night, but since the dream, his anger, coupled with the drawing of the scent, drove him to murder repeatedly until the light of the sun began to kiss the night sky and drive him into hiding.

It was a catastrophe for the Family of Loved Ones.

It became terribly difficult for Ira Stone and the other sector leaders to obtain the pureblood they needed, and Stone had to go to the Father to ask for his provision, which was granted. A black-market connection was provided by what appeared to be an accident. Then, each week like clockwork, the blood was delivered to each and every sector. For the time being, anyway, the Loved Ones were safe, and they were not hungry.

Because of this Mason felt no pull of guilt from his

former Family. Their hearts, which at one time had been united, had severed all ties with Stout, and he knew this full well, and he found he didn't care at all. He didn't allow himself the luxury of missing the past, not when he was so strong in the present. Let them bow down to the Dark Father as they wished. Mason had decided the world should be bowing down to him alone, even if murder was the only dictatorial and horrible way he would get the job done.

But there was one thing, aside from all the rest, which weighed heavily on him, almost driving him to the point of suffocation. Someone, or something, was seeking him out. He could not smell the thing; he could only sense it. He knew it did not know where he was, but he also knew it was searching, diligently, and it would not be deterred until it found him.

This drove him mad during the daylight hours when he was holed up all alone. He would try to fall into the peaceful sleep he'd had when he was active in the Family, but thoughts of this unseen pursuit plagued him like a wretched sickness. It caused him to toss and turn and dream of his own destruction day after day. He would wake out of breath, terrified, with salty tears running down his face and sweat all over his dead body. He was tormented with what he knew were things to come.

This was where Mason Stout was torn. He longed to be the strongest, the one being worshipped and catered to when it came to his kind, and, unhindered, he knew he could accomplish that task. But this thing which chased him… something inside of him knew beyond a shadow of a doubt that it would not allow him to reach his passionate goal.

So, the bodies of the murdered living continued to turn up, here and there, drained of all their blood, and sometimes, if they were women, raped as well. This was another horror he had been indulging in: the satisfaction of his newfound sexual appetites with a warm, living woman. They were never cooperative, so he simply made them.

Curfews had been established for both Philadelphia and Pittsburgh. While this did make things a bit more difficult, there were always those who defied this temporary law, so the sex was easy to find. It was more difficult to answer the call of the scent that drew him nightly. Many of those were locked up tight in their homes, and Stout had to do a bit of breaking and entering in order to get the blood he smelled.

But he did it.

Now he was perched high in a massive old oak tree near a park in Philly, and he was watching the entire area with his keen vision. The area, as far as he could tell, was empty. He had already killed for the night, and he was in no mood to continue. He didn't even feel the desire to find a woman. No, he was distracted. Distracted by the thing that sought him.

Tonight he could really feel it; it was very strong. Things like this made him desire the Father's approval once again. If he had it, he could go to him and ask that his hunter is executed. But he knew in his sick mind that the thing that looked for him was likely appointed by the Dark Father himself. Mason Stout was fully aware that he had lost full control long ago. He was no longer a Loved One. Now he was one of the hated, an abomination.

He closed his eyes and threw his head back, inhaling the scent of the night deeply. What was that smell that was always on his heels? It was determination. It was fury. It was murder.

Indeed, someone was on the tail of the vampire Mason Stout.

∞

Ira and Thorne sat in Stone's home office. It was early evening; there was a fire burning in the fireplace, and a few candles burned around them. Both men sat in silence, sipping cognac and waiting. With the Dark Father, waiting was the same as worship.

Ira had spoken with Thorne about the chosen Sasha Hunter.

"She is looking for him, and she is so well prepared for the moment she finds him," he had said. "But she is not even close to discovering where he is. I want to ask the Father to tell me where Stout is staying, where he is hiding, and I want to know if I can finally meet her. Even if the Father doesn't tell us where he is hiding, our meeting will make it easier. I can sniff the demon out."

Thorne had agreed to ask, and he did, right there in Ira's office. Now it was a matter of relaxing and waiting for their answer. They had been waiting for two hours, but it may as well have been days. The Dark Father would answer when he chose; no sooner, but definitely no later.

Mostly, they sat in silence, but every now and then one of them would speak. Mostly it was Ira; between waiting on the word of the devil and filling in at Stone & Kimble for Ira, Thorne was exhausted. So Ira, in an effort to break up the monotony, would ask him about things at the office, or how he was sleeping, if at all.

Ira Stone was busy himself. He spent almost all of his nights and days hovering around Sasha Hunter, watching her and listening to the thoughts in her mind. He had given her a few bits of advice, whispering them in her ear as she slept. One had been the silver finger caps; the other had been to tip the stakes with silver. Ira knew, that when the battle finally came, Stout would not know what hit him. But first Sasha would have to gain the upper hand, and it was there that the challenge could be found.

But there were no questions now, only waiting. Waiting for word from the Father. Waiting for his permission to advance. Ira knew he could count on the fact that the Father would see to it that Mason was stopped. Ira didn't have to worry about that. But the fact remained that he wanted things to go a bit faster, and the Father wasn't having any of that. Chances were that he was making Ira wait like this just to hone his patience a small bit, and it was working.

Another hour passed before Thorne Braun jerked hard and became rigid, dropping his brandy snifter to the floor, shattering it.

"The Father says, 'Why are you coming to me again so soon?' ", Thorne began. "Do you not trust that when the time to meet the girl is right, he will let you know?"

Ira put his own glass on the table, fearful that his persistence had angered the Dark Father. "Of course, Father. I am aware. It seems that she is struggling to locate him, and I only want to help."

"Silence!" So loudly did this come from Thorne's mouth that Ira began to tremble, humbled. "You do not only want to help, but you also want things done according to your weak little clock! Things work as I direct, not you!"

"Yes, Father. Forgive, forgive!"

Thorne, whose eyes were closed, shook his head and smiled. "Do you not know? I do not forgive; I move on. Only the God in Heaven forgives, and I am not him. I destroy."

"Yes. Yes!"

Thorne paused for a long moment before continuing. "I do grow weary of your groveling, Dark Dominant, and I am aware of your pure intentions when it comes to the Loved Ones. Therefore, here is your answer: yes, you may approach the girl. She is not to know what you are, and she is not to know a single, solitary thing about the Family. Approach her as a kindred spirit. Tell what lies you must as to why you want to 'team up,' as you would say, but you must do no more than advise. She must take care of Mason. She must kill him out of a spirit of revenge, or I will not accept him.

"Ira Stone, if it happens any other way, I will rip out what is left of your soul in exchange for his lost one."

Thorne Braun went limp; the Father had nothing more to say. Ira sat in his chair, shaking and waiting for his assistant to come to. It took more than a half-hour. The poor boy was literally exhausted.

Ira looked at him and smiled weakly. "I have my answer, Thorne, and I know what to do. Go home and rest; you will need plenty for the new week."

With that, Ira began to plan his first face-to-face encounter with Sasha Hunter.

R.W.K. Clark

# CHAPTER 19

Sasha Hunter rose at the crack of dawn, eager to begin her workout.

She put herself through a strict weight regimen, followed by a full half-hour of kickboxing, and finished her time off with a series of self-defense moves. She practiced on a heavy dummy that was attached to a strong, upright bar. It was satisfying and invigorating, and one of her favorite things about waking up each day.

But now it was time to shower. As she washed her body and hair, she went over self-defense moves in her head. She didn't even think about her art or other interests anymore; she had entered a realm of obsession that most people only read about in books. The funny thing was that her state, while she was aware of it, pleased her to no end. It kept her mind from the fact that she was alone in her life-long home; it made her forget that she had lost the person she loved most in the world.

It made her focus on what was truly important now.

Once she was dressed and groomed, Sasha grabbed up a short grocery list she had made up the night before from its place on the kitchen counter. Time to get something to eat, and start her search for the murdering mayor of Philly. She had stopped driving when this all began, in exchange for walking. It was better for her new, finely tuned body, and it always helped her to think more clearly.

As she walked to the store, she allowed herself to think about her father and the wonderful provision he had made for her in the event of his death. Not only did she have her now-forsaken college fund, but she also had insurance money she had received when he died. Sasha had never been a flagrant spender, so she had more than enough for anything she needed. But the truth of the matter was that she needed very little. Food, water, clothing, and a roof over her head, and she had all those things.

She took the main route to the grocery store and spent time going over the labels of every food item she bought. Her mother, who had passed when she was twelve, had taught her the importance of being careful what you put into your body. She used to say that if people had their health, they could deal with everything else. Sasha agreed in full with her mother, and she used to nag her father incessantly about his love for all things processed. It made her smile to think of him preparing his beloved bologna sandwiches for work each day.

Once her groceries were paid for and bagged up, she headed for home, strolling more than anything. It was a gorgeous fall day; colorful leaves were falling all around, and the temperature was a perfect sixty-eight degrees.

The sun shone brightly all around her, and it seemed she could hear the song of every single bird in existence. Sasha thought she would cut through the park on her way home, and perhaps she would even sit for a short time and enjoy the day before she began her daily pursuit.

She sat on a bench, two handled sacks of groceries next to her. The sun felt so good. It seemed she spent so much time in the darkness lately that she didn't reap enough of the sun's benefits. Sasha closed her eyes and turned her face to the sky to soak in as much of it as she could.

"Don't you just love the feel of the warm sun on your face, young lady?"

Her eyes flew open, and her hand went up to block the light from her line of vision. A man stood before her; he looked to be in his early sixties, with a full head of white hair cut neatly and stylishly. He wore newer-looking blue jeans and a hooded sweatshirt with a t-shirt visible beneath. He was smiling, and the smile reached his blue eyes and added to them generously. The man reminded her, painfully, of her dear father.

"Yes, I do," she replied, returning his smile. "I was just thinking that I don't get out in it nearly enough."

"May I sit?" he asked as he motioned toward the empty spot in the bench. She nodded and moved her bags, putting them between the two of them. He took a seat and put his face toward the sun as she had. "It even seems to clear out the sinuses. Smell that beautiful air!" Now he opened his eyes and turned to her, his smile remaining. "There was a substantial time in my life when I didn't get enough sun either, but those days are behind me now."

Sasha smiled back, but she was wary; you had to be these days. You couldn't trust everyone you met. After they sat in silence for a moment, she took her bags by the handles and said, "I guess I'd better be going; I have a busy day ahead."

"Yes," he replied. "Do you work?"

Suddenly, Sasha felt the overwhelming urge to just talk. Talk to someone, even if it was a strange old man in the park. She let her hands drop back into her lap.

"No," she said. "Actually, I recently had a death in my family, and my focus has been a little… off, if you know what I mean."

"I'm sorry," he replied. "Do you mind if I ask?"

Tears began to well up in her eyes, and she fought them back. "No. My father. My father was killed by the guy doing the vampire killings."

The man remained silent for a long moment, waiting patiently to hear anything more she might want to say. When it became apparent to him that she would not speak, he said, "My name is Ira Stone. What's yours?"

Sasha immediately held her hand out toward him. "Sasha Hunter."

"Ah, I believe I heard about your father's death," he said as they shook. "You see, I am one of the heads of Stone & Kimble Pharmaceuticals. We currently have a contract with GenetiLabs, where your father worked. I am so very sorry, Sasha."

"Me, too."

Ira crossed his arms over his chest and sat back on the bench. He looked around briefly, feeling full well that her eyes were on his every move. "I am livid beyond disbelief over the murders. Do you believe in real vampires, Sasha?"

She didn't answer, but she nodded slowly.

"I mean, even existing before this supposed 'poison blood'?" he continued.

She nodded yet again.

"Why do you believe, Sasha?" he asked.

She thought for a moment about her words, her eyes scanning his face, looking for the safety and security she would need to really talk to him. Finally, she decided to take a small risk. She would tell him, but only just a little.

"After it happened," she began, "my father's murder, I mean, I started to do a bit of research into Mayor Stout's background. Let's just say I became a believer."

Now Ira Stone sat forward a bit. He looked around conspiratorially once again, then turned to her and said in a low voice, "What did it? What convinced you?"

It was hard for her to answer; what she was about to say sounded insane, even to her. But what was this guy going to do, have her committed? She had nothing to lose by sharing, and she knew it.

"Well, he claimed to have been born to Tiberius Stout of Genesee," she shared. "But then his parents were killed and yadda, yadda, yadda. It all sounded believable, but only on the surface, like a finely crafted fairy tale. Then I found the article; it was written by a newspaper to announce what he claimed to be his birth."

Ira sat back and crossed his arms again. "Go on."

"It'll sound nuts," she said shyly.

He smiled at her. "Do you believe it?"

"Yes."

"Then so will I," he confirmed.

Sasha took a deep breath. "The article was in two parts, with two photographs. The first part talked about little Mason being named for his great-great-grandfather, Mason Joseph Stout. It seemed, according to the mayor's father, that this Mason disappeared, never to be heard from again. His family was killed, all except one boy, Tiberius' great-grandfather. So the mayor was named in the older man's honor."

Ira nodded. "Interesting."

"Well," she continued. "None of that made me question anything. Until the second half of the article, that is."

"And?"

"There was a second photograph. This one showed Tiberius holding a photo of the great-great Mason." She stopped and looked down at her feet. She couldn't believe she was talking to this stranger about this. "It was Mason Stout, the mayor, in that photo."

Ira Stone gave her no response for a while. Finally, he asked, "What makes you so sure?"

"The math and the circumstances. Young Mason

disappeared when his parents burned up at the textile mill they owned. Suddenly, just before running for mayor, he pops back up." She smiled to herself, feeling surer than ever. "It is what it is, Mr. Stone, and it's what I believe to be true."

Ira broke into laughter. No wonder the Dark Father had chosen this girl to rein in the defiant one. No one in the world had caught those discrepancies in Stout's story, and they had always existed in print. She was paying attention, and she was smart as a whip.

"Very good, Miss Sasha Hunter," he told her. "Very good indeed."

Sasha knit her brow with confusion. "What do you mean?"

"I run a company which focuses on healing and curing people, young Sasha," Ira began. "When the initial robbery at GenetiLabs happened, I was the first to find out what had been stolen. Then, when the rash of murders began, I decided it was time to find some things out for myself, and I discovered the same things. I believe the man has always been a vampire. I want him stopped before any more humans have to die."

The lies came easily for Ira Stone; the Dark Father would be exceedingly pleased.

Sasha was really studying him now. "How would you stop him?" she asked. She was feeling him out, and Ira knew it, of course.

"Well, dear, if I were twenty years younger, or more I would hunt the evil menace down and drive a stake through his heart," he said. "They say it's one of the best ways if he really is a vampire. Even if I'm wrong, and he isn't, it would kill any human being alive. The world would be rid of one murderous, bloodthirsty devil, that's for sure. But, alas, I have neither the strength nor the stamina."

Silence took over their conversation once again. Ira watched her carefully as she sat, staring at her hands and thinking hard. It didn't take long for her to spill her soul to him, and he was so very relieved.

"I am going to do it, you know. I am going to kill Mason Stout."

She was still looking at her hands, wringing them slightly. Ira was still looking at her, and he was smiling. "This is a monstrous task you are assuming. Do you realize what you are saying?"

"Yes," she replied quietly. "And I am ready to die if need be."

"What if he turns you into one like himself? Then what?"

She looked up at him, her face and eyes as serious as he had ever seen. "I will throw myself headlong on a stake tipped in silver."

"So," he asked, "what is keeping you from this immense, yet justified, goal of yours?"

Sasha shrugged and began to look around the park; she was getting a bit anxious. "I am prepared; I have the perfect weapons, ones I created myself. When I find him, I will send him back to the abyss he came from. But… I have to find him first."

Now it was Ira's turn to look around. As the Dark

Father said, he must speak after careful thought, and he must not divulge too much. It took him only a moment to settle on his words.

"What if I use my resources to find him, and you use your strength to do him in, Sasha?"

Now he had her attention in full. She turned to look at him, her eyes wide and anxious. She spoke so fast her words nearly ran together.

"You know where Mason Stout is?"

Ira shook his head. "No, I didn't say that. I said I have resources, and those resources will lead us right to him. We simply must work together. You see, I am too old for the battle, but the search is right up my alley. I want him dead too, Sasha. As long as he lives, the lives of everyone are at risk."

"I need to think about this," she replied nervously. This was simply too easy, and too good to be true. Where did this guy come from, anyway? She took hold of the handles on her plastic grocery bags. "My food is going to spoil; I've been out too long, and I need to get it home."

"I understand," he said. "But I think you'll find that the food will be in top condition, dear." He pulled a business card from the front pocket of his hoodie. "Here. Just in case you decide in my favor."

Sasha took the card and looked it over. 'Ira Stone, President and CEO, Stone & Kimble Pharmaceuticals.' These words were followed by the company address and Stone's personal cell phone number. She tucked the card into the back pocket of her jeans.

"I'll do some thinking, and probably a bit of research also," she told him. "I'll be in touch either way, Mr. Stone." Sasha stood and adjusted her bags in her hands. "Oh, and thank you for listening without judging."

"All of us will be judged, Sasha," he said quietly. "And it is not my job to do it."

She began to walk away briskly. When she was about fifty feet from the bench she turned to offer the man a smile, but he was gone, and he was nowhere to be seen. She continued home, her mind on the man at the bench who had so easily believed and understood her.

Sasha Hunter knew in her heart she would call him before the night was upon her; there would be no research needed.

# CHAPTER 20

Mason Stout sat on the edge of his bed at the hotel. The sun was still up, but the sky was orange from the approaching night. He hadn't been able to enter his rest all day, and that fact made him edgy and angry.

The fact was that he had fallen asleep for a bit when he first lay on his bed at daybreak, but when he entered into his dream state, he ran into it again.

This time he was not on a bench; he was fleeing for his life. He would run the streets and take to the sky, but no matter how fast he went or how far, as soon as he stopped the thing was there, waiting to rip his dead, beating heart out of his chest. In the dream, he felt terrified, hopeless, and hunted.

He wasn't able to stop the scream from coming when it sank its clawed hand into his chest. He awoke to his own shrieks, and it took him a full thirty seconds to regain his waking composure and put his own hand over his mouth, but it was too late.

There was a pounding at the door to his room. Mason looked at the clock frantically, it was only eleven in the morning. He jumped up, glad for the heavy draperies protecting him from the sun.

"Yes? Who's there?"

"Housekeeping, Mr. Stanley," came the female voice. "Is everything okay in there? Can I get you anything?"

He had been furious. "Do you not see the sign on the knob?"

"Yessir, but…"

"No, thank you," he said loudly in an aggravated tone. "Now go away!"

When he was sure that she was gone Mason plopped down on the bed, his emotions stirred and his mind a jumble. That had been hours ago, and he had been sitting in much the same way ever since, waiting for the dark blanket of the night to come over the sky and protect him once again.

He needed to wash his body. He reeked of sweat; it had soaked into the sheets, permeating them and making them intolerable. Now he wished he had asked the maid to leave sheets outside the door. He picked up the telephone receiver and requested that some be left for him, along with clean towels. Soon, Mason was standing beneath icy water, scrubbing at his body with a soapy cloth. He hoped the cold water would cool his searing soul.

By the time he had dressed and combed his hair, it was time to leave. A scent had come to him; he could tell it was male, and he was disappointed. His dreams as of late had him so frazzled that he was afraid to pursue a second victim, even if only for the sex. Something inside of him told him to put such silly urges out of his mind. He would hunt once, and do it just for the thrill. Then, he thought he might perch atop one of the bridges and just watch the sky until it began to turn gold along the edges.

He took a bag of blood out of the refrigerator. There was only one left after this one; tomorrow night he would have to go out again. Mason was at the point that he didn't think he could live without this special treat, even for one day. The very thought of doing so hurt his skin and brought tears to his eyes. He was like a junkie with only one fix left.

He drank his bag for the night and reveled in the high it brought him. Feeling empowered and very energetic, Mason Stout flung his window open and took off into the black night, all thoughts of his dream and his exhaustion gone. Now he was driven, a predator with a purpose, strong and sharp.

If anyone tried to hunt him, he would drain them dry.

∞

Ira stood alone in his den at his home. He was at the bar pouring rich scotch over tiny, perfect little ice cubes, and he was humming along as he did so. Since making contact with the stubborn and determined Sasha Hunter, Ira felt a newfound freedom from his fears for the Family of Loved Ones.

But now she must call him. What if she didn't? He had thought to himself a number of times, but he knew she would. It was the will of the Dark Father, and it was his job to motivate her to move in the direction he desired. All Ira needed to do was wait, without worry, for the chiming of his phone. So, he did the very best he could to do just that.

At six-thirty, Harvey, his houseboy, brought him a delicious meal of rare lamb, baby potatoes, and garden-fresh roasted carrots. He enjoyed it with a nice glass of burgundy, and the entire feast helped him to relax even more. One of the best things about the gift the Father had given them was their ability to enjoy the food of the living once again; what a wonderful extravagance!

For dessert, he had a simple ice cream with blueberries on top, and after that, he went back to his den to wait. She would call; he knew it. It just seemed to be taking her forever to do so.

No sooner had the thought crossed his mind than his cell phone rang. He looked at the screen, which read 'Sasha Hunter.' He had already gotten the number and programmed it in. When he saw her name on the screen, he had to smile. What an appropriate surname Hunter was.

"Hello, this is Ira Stone," he said in a warm tone.

There was a pause. "Mr. Stone, this is Sasha. I met you at the park today, remember?"

"Sasha!" he said warmly. "What a pleasant surprise!"

"Um, I'm not sure I should have done this," she began, "but did you mean what you said about helping me, sir?"

He could hear her desperation, and it broke his heart. She reminded him so much of his daughter Ellie. She had died in 1842 from tuberculosis, and she had been his favorite of all time.

"I absolutely and positively meant it, dear."

He could hear her breathe a sigh of relief. "Okay, good. So, what's next, Mr. Stone?"

"Next, my dear girl, you call me Ira." He couldn't help but chuckle. "Get some rest tonight; you are going to need it. We will meet at Wanda's Café for breakfast at eight thirty in the morning."

"Shouldn't I go out tonight?"

"No, dear," he replied reassuringly. "Chances are we will locate him almost right away, and you may not get to sleep for a while. Trust me, Sasha."

They said their goodbyes, and he hung up.

Now he rose and poured himself another scotch. Well, Stout, Ira thought, I hope you have your fun tonight, because it will be the last good time you ever have on this Earth. He smiled at his thoughts as he poured his drink.

Now, he could rest through the night. He would meet the girl in the morning, and by tomorrow evening the hunt would begin. But it wouldn't be much of a hunt, for now that Ira had the Dark Father's permission to find Stout, Ira could use his strong senses. He might not be as strong as Stout physically, but his senses were in incredible condition.

He would sniff the nuisance out in no time at all; it was the girl who would need all the strength she could get.

# CHAPTER 21

Sasha's alarm went off while it was still dark, as usual.

She stumbled directly to the basement to get in her normal workout. Now was not the time to slack off; she had a feeling deep in her guts that all of this was going to come to a head sooner rather than later. She wanted to be in the best shape possible.

She thought about Ira Stone while she worked. She'd called him, but she still had her doubts when she laid her head on her pillow. Sasha knew that if this was the wrong thing to do, then sleeping on it was the wisest. Her stomach would tell her, as soon as she opened her eyes, to back off, but it did not. If anything, it validated her decision, and now she was getting eager to move.

Once she was finished, she showered and dressed, thinking only of Mason Stout and his demise. The thought of seeing him face to face and engaging him in battle gave her a tingling feeling in her stomach that spread throughout her body. Was that nerves? Yes, mixed with a bit of fear for her own life, but that was only natural. The fact was that if she died battling the monster, she would welcome it. With her father gone, she truly had no desire to live anyway. If she was victorious, what would the next step of her life be?

Ready to go at last, Sasha drank the remainder of coffee from her cup and rinsed it out before placing it in the dish drainer. She then grabbed her wallet and cell phone and stepped out into the bright sun of a new day. The morning air was fresh and invigorating, and she inhaled its power and scent deeply into her lungs before locking and closing the front door of her home.

Time to start a brand-new day.

∞

"I'd like a coffee, black, and some rye toast with butter, please."

Sasha placed her order and looked across the booth at Ira Stone. He offered her a brief smile before placing his own. "Two eggs over medium with ham and hash browns," he said. "Oh, yes, and coffee with cream and sugar."

"Cream and sugar are right there on your table, honey." The red-haired waitress winked at the older gentleman before turning away to put in their order.

Once she was a good distance away, Sasha leaned forward. "So, Mr. Stone, what is the first order of business?"

"The first order of business would be for you to get it into your head that you need to call me Ira," he retorted. "I truly insist. I think a first-name basis is appropriate, considering what we are engaged in together, don't you, Sasha?"

She grinned and blushed slightly. "If my father heard me call one of my elders by the first name, he would have my hide," she said. "But yes, I would have to agree it is… appropriate."

"Good," he replied. The waitress brought two cups of hot coffee and set them before the pair. "Thank you," Ira told her with a smile, and she walked away. "Now, here is where I am. You called a bit late last evening for me to tap my resources regarding Stout's whereabouts. But now that I know this is all a go, I will be spending my daylight hours doing just that: locating him."

"Why not now?" Sasha asked. "I mean, why can't we go together, and when you find him I simply fight him then and there?"

Ira shook his head. "We need to know where he is holed up; this is a process. Listen, of course that would be ideal because he will be sleeping during the daylight hours. But advancing on him in the light of day would be dangerous for both of us, especially if you manage to take him out, which is the intention. It could mean prison for both of us. That may not mean much to you, but I run a major conglomeration, and it just isn't acceptable."

Sasha couldn't pretend to understand his reasoning altogether, but she accepted it. He was older and wiser, and she knew it, so she simply nodded and waited for him to continue. She was anxious to know all aspects of the plan.

"My resources are very dependable," he told her.

"They will be able to sniff him out before sundown, and of that, I am very confident. You said you have the weapons that you have been preparing yourself?"

"Yes, working out, designing the weapons, et cetera."

Ira nodded. "Tell me about them, dear."

The waitress returned, a plate in each hand. She set a small one before Sasha with toast on it. "Rye with butter, and…" Then she set Ira's down. "Eggs over medium, hash-brown potatoes, and ham. Anything else, you two?"

"No, thank you," he said with a smile. "This is perfect."

Sasha took a bite of her toast, swallowed it, and answered his question. "I designed a crossbow with silver-tipped arrows which will shoot them fast and consecutively. I made a silver sword, learned to use a lasso in case I have the opportunity to pull him into the sun, and I have been working out to the point of exhaustion." She took another bite. "Oh, and my favorite: silver finger blades that fit right on the tips of my fingers. You would have to see them to believe them. They are pretty darn cool."

Ira smiled. She couldn't possibly know that he had whispered these ideas to her as she slept, or that he had been keeping an eye on her for quite some time. The truth of the matter was that she was more than prepared to take on the monster that was Mason Stout. As a matter of fact, with him in her corner, she had a very good chance of coming out on top. The Dark Father would reward her well, even if she weren't a follower. She was doing his work, after all.

"It sounds like you have all of your ducks in a row, dear," he told her. "Now, as soon as I track him down, and I mean immediately, I will be calling you. I will fetch you in my vehicle, and we will make our way to him together. I may not be able to fight him myself, but I will certainly not leave you on your own."

"Why are you doing this, Ira?" she asked him. "There is more to it than the fact that GenetiLabs was robbed. I know it."

He got a thoughtful look on his face, as though he were weighing his words. "We were members of the same church, as were a number of his victims. Let's just say I consider taking him out to be the Father's work."

Sasha accepted this with no further questions. It made perfect sense to her mind, even if she didn't understand it was the Dark Father Ira was referring to. It really didn't matter; the job was going to get done, and she was the one chosen to do it.

The pair ate their breakfasts in silence, then, while they waited for the check that Ira insisted on paying, Sasha told him about her father. She shared how the man had worked his fingers to the bone to be both mother and father to her, and she shared fond memories of the good times she'd had with him. Ira could feel her heartbreak, and it enraged him. This was a good girl who suddenly found herself alone in the world because of one of his old sector leaders, and Ira Stone was going to see to it that things were made right for her.

With the check paid, the two of them stepped out into the sunlight. "It's truly a beautiful day once again," she said. "I take it as a wonderful omen. Perhaps this signifies a new beginning for me. Maybe my life has hope."

"Of course it does," Ira said, putting an arm on her shoulder and giving her a fatherly squeeze. "You are going to get every ounce of closure you deserve, my dear. Every single ounce. Now, can I drive you home? I would like you to work out a bit more today, you know, just to be extra-prepared."

"I think I'll walk through the park, thanks," she replied. "And I intended to work out some more anyway. Brilliant minds think alike… Ira."

He nodded and smiled. "Indeed they do."

The old man climbed in his car and was off like a shot, leaving Sasha staring after him. She couldn't express in words how thankful she was for him being there to help, understanding her need to do what she had to do. It was strange that he was so willing, but if she really thought about it, she was sure that most of the state of Pennsylvania was hoping someone would do the exact same things. The police were failing, and the killings continued. While they were in the café, the people in the booth next to them were discussing a body found just that morning.

She started to head for home; there was no use crying over spilled milk.

# CHAPTER 22

Ira left Wanda's Café and went directly to Thorne Braun, who was already at Stone & Kimble signing a stack of paperwork for Ira in his absence. He found him sitting in a chair, the paperwork on a clipboard and a pen in his hand. Ira smiled and watched him for a moment in silence.

"Why are you not sitting at my desk, Thorne?"

Thorne didn't even look up. "I am not worthy to sit in your seat, and besides, I am comfortable right here. You cannot sneak in around me, sir. You realize I smelled you as soon as you pulled your car into the lot."

"Yes, I do realize it." The man sat at his desk. "I wanted to let you know that I will be spending the day doing a bit of sniffing myself. I will track down Stout, and hope for a confrontation tonight."

Thorne put the clipboard on an end table next to his chair. He looked up at Ira. "I am able to give you a bit of help. The Dark Father spoke to me regarding this."

"What did he say?" Ira asked eagerly.

Thorne stood and took a seat across the large desk from Ira. "Not much, I must admit, but I am sure it tells of Mason's location."

"Well?"

"He said only a single word, but he has repeated it to me all morning," Thorne said. "It is 'Tucktin.'"

A very confused look came over Ira's face. "Tucktin?"

"Yes sir. Tucktin."

Ira sat back in his chair, his brow knit and his mind racing. This was a very important thing that was going to be done, and it had been ordered by the Dark Father himself. Nothing he said to Thorne could be disregarded, no matter how confusing or seemingly nonsensical. Tucktin? What could that mean?

"Have you asked the Father for clarity on this… one word?" he asked Thorne.

Thorne nodded and smiled. "Of course I did. Twice. But all he would say to me in response was Tucktin."

"Well, then, there is something to it." Ira flipped open the laptop sitting on his desk and began a search of the word. "It would certainly help if I knew how it was spelled."

First, he looked to see if there was a small town, anywhere, named 'Tucktin,' and he tried variations of the spelling. He assumed it was a town, perhaps even spelled 'Tuckton,' but he had absolutely no luck with that search whatsoever. Next, he simply entered the word the way he assumed it was spelled, 'Tucktin,' along with the words 'Philadelphia,' 'Pittsburgh,' and 'Pennsylvania.'

The very first match that came up on his search engine told him everything he desired to know.

"Tucked Inn, a shabby little hotel on the west side from the looks of it Thorne," Ira read aloud with excitement. "That has to be it. The Tucked Inn."

He looked up at his assistant, but Thorne was sitting, his eyes closed and a calm look on his face. He was nodding peacefully, and he was smiling. That was it, Ira knew immediately. Mason Stout was holed up at a hotel called the 'Tucked Inn.'

He jotted the address down on the back of one of his business cards and put it in the pocket on the inside of his jacket. Standing, he said to Thorne, "This may not be it, but I have a very strong feeling it is. The Dark Father has not left us hanging. He has come through for the Loved Ones, just as he always does when we act in his will. I am going to go sniff the beast out."

Thorne didn't answer him; he simply sat with his eyes closed, still nodding. Ira shook his head and left the office, exhilarated. It wouldn't do to interrupt his assistant's reverie when he was communicating with the Father.

Time to pay a visit to the 'Tucked Inn.'

∞

The 'Tucked Inn' Hotel proved to be a worn-down brick building on West Montgomery Avenue. It sported an aged neon sign with the letter 'c' and one 'n' burned out on it, and lowlifes and street urchins hung out in the front in either dirty or scant clothing.

Ira Stone sat in the back of a taxi cab staring at the building. The driver was patient for about ten minutes, then demanded payment or to get back on the road; the day was wasting. Ira tossed a hundred-dollar bill at him and told him to keep the change. Suddenly the man was more than friendly.

Stone got out of the cab and immediately felt out of place. His cleaned pressed khakis, white collared shirt and black jacket gave him away: he didn't belong in this part of town. But Ira had never been one to let discomfort direct his steps; he wasn't afraid.

But it wasn't only the lack of fear which drove him on, it was also the scent of the renegade vampire Mason Stout filling his nose that kept him standing there. The menace was in there; the air reeked of him. Members of the Family could always identify one another by scent, just as dogs did, and Ira could clearly recall that of Stout. But now the smell was stronger, and it was filled with rot. He had definitely turned, and nothing about the transformation was good. No wonder the Dark Father recalled him to the Lower Realm.

Ira didn't hesitate for another minute and headed for the main door of the dive that towered before him. Heads turned, women began to whistle and make like they were going to sidle up and proposition him, and a couple of dirty men in torn-up clothing began to circle behind him. But Stone paid them no mind; neither they nor their intentions played a part in his mission, and he would not be distracted.

The single glass door which served as the main entrance was propped open with a piece of broken brick to let the air inside the lobby. Ira entered the shadowy, dingy space and looked around. There were several vinyl-covered waiting chairs and rusty metal end tables. There were also a few tall, circular ashtrays, and disheveled people, both men, and women, were seated at them, puffing away and flicking their ashes on the floor beside them.

To the right was an enclosure with glass all around the upper part of it. A dirty man with sweat stains on the armpits of his filthy white shirt and a nappy beard sat looking at a copy of an adult magazine. Ira's face cringed in disgust. He approached a window in the glass and tapped on the desk bell located there.

The man looked up immediately. He offered Ira a smile and shook his head. After a moment of this, he stood and ambled to the window, sliding it open forcefully.

"No vacancies," he said gruffly, the smile never leaving his face.

Ira smiled back sarcastically, using only half his mouth. "I'm not here to rent a room. I'm looking for my long-lost brother."

"Oh, really?" the man replied with feigned wonder. "I didn't know cops had long-lost brothers."

Now Ira roared with laughter, and he did it extra-loudly, for effect. "I'm no damn cop, you idiot." He stared into the man's eyes, entrancing him into silence. "I said, I'm looking for my long-lost brother. His name is Mason Stout."

It took a moment for the man to answer him. He first had to snap out of the trance Ira had put him in, and even when he did, he was unable to stop staring stupidly. Stone found it slightly entertaining.

The man finally responded in a low, monotone voice. "No Mason Stout here."

"Well, that's fine," Ira replied. "I'm sure you won't mind if I just stroll through the place and see, now do you?"

The guy shook his head slowly. "No problem, sir. Take your time."

"Thanks."

Ira walked away, heading for the elevator, but he didn't plan to use it. Next to it was the door to the fire stairs, and that was exactly what he would use. He would go by smell, and using the stairs would make it so much easier. Besides, when he reached the elevator, it opened up, and an old man came out. It reeked of sex and sweat, and the inside looked as if the thing would drop down the shaft at any moment.

There were no rooms on the first floor from what he could see; just a rec room with a busted-up pool table and a couple of restrooms and other doors with locks, but no numbers. Onward and upward, Ira thought.

He took the stairs and opened the door to the second floor. A haggard old woman was struggling with her key, but the rest of the corridor was empty. The balding, stained carpet was giving off a smell that gagged him, but Mason's scent was still too weak; he wasn't on that floor.

On the third floor, he had the same luck; the only difference was a junkie crouched beneath a payphone shooting up. Ira winced with disgust and headed up to the fourth and final floor, letting the door on the third slam shut. Best to put the last eyeful far behind him.

As soon as he opened the door to the fourth floor, the smell of Stout hit him so hard he actually had to jerk his head back to get away from the stench. He stepped into the corridor and closed his eyes, and he began to slowly breathe in and out. It was best to get used to the scent immediately; he would have to deal with it until the beast met his demise.

There were ten rooms on the floor, five on each side of the corridor. This particular hall suffered from many burned-out lightbulbs, the sound of droning flies, and was bare of carpeting. Ira walked softly on the worn floor so as to not cause heavy footsteps. If he were lucky Stout would be in his rest, and footsteps wouldn't matter; the only things able to rouse a resting vampire were exposure to sun, nightmares, or Satan himself.

He passed each door slowly, but he knew instinctively that Stout was in none of them. What encouraged him was the fact that with each step he took the scent became stronger and stronger. Finally, he stood before the last door on the right: room 410.

The stench emanating from within burned his nostrils; the menace was inside. Ira Stone was willing to bet he was sleeping, or Stout would have smelled him and met him where he stood. Stone put his ear carefully to the door and listened.

Faintly, ever so faintly, he could hear the restful breathing of the former mayor of Philadelphia, Mason

Stout.

Ira closed his eyes and tried to tap into Stout's mind, but it seemed the animal had some kind of wall up. This proved to Ira how distant he truly was from both the Father and the gift he had bestowed on the Loved Ones. Had there been anything left to salvage, Ira would have been able to read him, even ever so slightly. But there was nothing.

He stepped back from the door and stared at it for a long moment. What should the next step be? Hopefully, he would sleep until sunset. What were his plans at that point? It would be important to know.

Ira snapped out of his own mind and looked around. If he were correct in his sense of direction, the window to Stout's room would face West Washington, the very street he had been sitting on in the taxi. At nightfall, he and Sasha could sit in the car and wait for Stout to come out of the door of the hotel.

If he didn't stay true to old-fashioned bloodsucker form and use his window.

But it didn't matter if he did; they would be able to keep an eye on that as well from the street. Ira would rent an older model car for cheap because Mason knew all of his vehicles. After all, he knew them all well. There was a time when the two of them had actually been friends.

But to Ira Stone, those memories seemed like unreal dreams as he stood in the hall breathing in Stout's stench.

After countless minutes passed, Ira stepped back

and turned to go back to the staircase. He would go home and get his own simple sedan and proceed to rent a vehicle. Then, he would return, have lunch, and give Sasha Hunter the call he knew she was anxiously awaiting.

As he took the stairs, he dialed up a taxi on his cell phone and picked up his step. He could hardly wait to share the good news and let that tough cookie of a girl know that all was ready. He hoped she didn't let her fear stop what had to happen.

But the Dark Father would never let anything get in the way of his will.

# CHAPTER 23

It was nearly two o'clock in the afternoon before the terribly nervous Sasha gave in and sat down to put something in her growling stomach. She didn't get too extravagant, though. She chose a repeat of her breakfast, only with milk this time: rye toast with butter. As she sat at the table chewing, she thought about Ira Stone and wondered if he was having any luck locating Stout.

The girl was nearly halfway through with her second slice when her cell rang obnoxiously, startling her and causing her to drop her toast. Sasha jumped up and grabbed the phone, which sat on the kitchen counter. She swiped the screen with her finger and saw the name 'Mr. Stone'.

"Hello?"

"Hello, Sasha," he greeted her. "How has your day been? How was your workout?"

She took a breath to relieve the anxiety she felt. "My workout was great, but I have been pacing all day waiting for your call. I can't help it, I guess. Have you had any luck finding Stout?"

He didn't answer right away, and Sasha was holding her breath when her heart sank. As though he were reading her mind and visualizing her disappointment, Ira finally chuckled lightly.

"No worries, Sasha dear," he said. "I have located Mason Stout, just as I promised you I would."

"Where is he? Tell me!"

"Now, now, don't get ahead of yourself," he said in a parental tone. "If I told you now you would rush off and not have the guidance from me that you need to save your own life."

Sasha closed her eyes in resignation. "You're right, Ira. I would. So, what's the plan?"

"The sun sets tonight at seven-sixteen in the evening, but it won't be quite dark enough for him to advance," he continued. "Even the slightest sunlight glimmering on the horizon would be enough to harm him, likely blinding him, and I can promise you he is fully aware of that. I expect him to play it safe and attempt to leave around a half-hour to forty-five minutes later. But I will pick you up at six-thirty. We must be there before he leaves."

"What do you want me to do?" she asked him in nothing more than a whisper.

Ira paused, then said, "Be ready, dear. Just be very ready."

With that, their call ended. Sasha stared at the phone only for a few seconds before placing it back on the counter and walking directly to the basement, to her workout area and to the weapons she had made. She spent the next several hours doing nothing but priming her body for what was to come, and though she had no way of knowing what that would be, she did know it had the potential to produce great disaster in her life if she didn't take what she was going to do very seriously.

She picked up her weapons and put them on her body just as she intended. A belt with a sheathed sword on her left and a lasso on her right. Her silver-bladed fingertips went on her fingers, and she finally picked up her crossbow.

It was time to begin her workout yet again.

∞

Ira Stone pulled into Sasha's driveway at exactly six twenty-nine that evening. He sat in his car after honking a single time, waiting for her to come out, and he stared at the small, modest home she lived in. He could feel the sorrow which poured out from under the door and through the cracked windows. The girl was living a nightmare of Mason Stout's making, and tonight she would have her revenge.

The revenge of the Dark Father.

He had to wait only about two minutes. She appeared at the front door with her weapons on her, but she made sure to look out into the street and up and down it. There was no one out there; everyone was petrified to show their faces at night, and it was quickly coming. They were safely locking themselves inside their homes, drawing the blinds, and turning out the lights.

After securing the house, Sasha approached Ira's rental sedan and climbed in, but she couldn't help but notice the shabby state of the vehicle: rust, a couple of minor dents, and paint chips missing here and there. She got in and began to attempt to buckle her seatbelt around her awkward gear.

"Tell me you don't own this car," she said to Ira with a smile.

He grinned and put the car in reverse. "Rental. You are funny, Sasha Hunter."

Soon they were off, and by five minutes of seven they were parked across the street from the 'Tucked Inn' Hotel, the engine off and the lights out. Ira had the windows up so they couldn't be heard conversing by the ingrates who seemed to be coming out of the woodwork. He would send anyone packing who tried to converse with them in any manner, and he had the power to do so.

"Okay, Sasha," he began. "That is the main door." He pointed with his forefinger. "I do not, I repeat, do not, expect Mason Stout to use this entrance, but he may. See, he would have been recognized at check-in, so he must have been in disguise. Who knows how he got it done? Anyway, when he leaves he will be fast; he will be trying to hurry to accomplish whatever he has planned for the evening. I expect him to leave flying."

"You mean 'in the air' flying?"

Ira nodded and turned to her. "Exactly." He turned his attention back to the building and pointed again. "See the last window on the top floor there? It is lit up; he is awake. That is his window."

Sasha stared, and suddenly she was overwhelmed with the knowledge that Mason Stout was literally across the street from her.

"I am going to be honest with you," Ira continued. "I fully expect him to take flight from the window. Doing that, there is little chance anyone will take notice of his comings and goings, and that is how he wants it. I will watch the window because I am behind the wheel. You watch the main door. If he does happen to exit at the door, simply say, 'There he is,' and we will be on his tail. Understand?"

Sasha nodded nervously. "Yes."

So, the pair sat in silence, watching and waiting. At ten minutes after seven Sasha said, "I'm a little scared, Ira."

"I know you are, dear," he replied softly.

She took a breath. "Do you think I can do this?"

"I already know you can, and you will."

She listened to his words carefully and let their power sink into her soul. She repeated them to herself over and over: 'I can and I will.' Soon, her hands were no longer shaking, and her breathing was calm once more. It was the last shred of doubt she would have.

At seven forty the game suddenly changed.

"There he is!" Ira said in a harsh whisper.

Sasha's eyes went to the last window on the top floor just in time to see the man throwing up the sash. He flew from the window and into the night sky so suddenly that it took her breath away. She opened her mouth to tell Ira to 'go!', but he was already gone, the car in gear and following.

"I lost him with my eyes," Sasha told him after only

a minute on the road.

"No," Ira replied. "I see him. Keep looking and you will too."

But the truth was that Ira had lost him, too. He didn't need to see him though; the stench coming off of that monster was filling his nostrils enough that he was keeping up, and it helped him to even spot his soaring now and again.

They drove for nearly ten minutes at a very high rate of speed, zigging and zagging and turning on a dime often. Suddenly, Ira saw him zip to the left, and as he prepared to turn left, he realized where they were. His eyes grew wide, but then he realized that this was perfect; it was the ideal place in which to end the life of Mason Stout.

"He is going to GenetiLabs," Ira said with a smile. "He must be out of blood."

Sasha turned to him in shock. "What do you mean, 'he's going to GenetiLabs'? Another guard will die!"

Ira turned quickly and accelerated; they were only two blocks from the place. "Perhaps. But he will die soon after. We have to keep our perspective. Now, listen to me: when we get there, you need to head in. I will be right on your tail, understand? The faster we act, the better the chance of saving whoever the guard is, understand?"

They approached the next corner, and GenetiLabs could be seen from there. Ira put out the headlights and pulled the car over and shut it off just in time to catch a glimpse of Stout landing on the roof of the building. He smiled.

"Go, Sasha," he told her with his hand on her arm. Remember all you have worked for, and use every last bit! I will be in behind you, but I want to stay out of his sight if I can. If for some reason you fail, he will come for my family."

Sasha looked at him, and suddenly something came to her heart: this man didn't want to be seen for another reason. She couldn't place it, and she trusted that he was on her side, but there was more to him that she first believed. She gave him a single nod and jumped from the vehicle; Ira softly closed the car door behind her.

Sasha hit the ground running. She darted through a bit of barren field, then across the single-lane street. She could see him on the roof, and then he disappeared, as if through some kind of shaft or crawlspace opening. Suddenly she saw a guard pacing back and forth at the side of the building. Sasha picked up her pace and ran at him with all she had.

When she reached him she said, "The vampire is here, and I am here to kill him. You must go! Let me in the building and go!"

The man looked at her, his mouth was agape. At first, she thought he might argue, but suddenly a dazed look came over his face, and he pulled a large ring of keys off his belt, slipped one into the door, and turned it, letting her in. She turned back to him, and in a harsh whisper said, "Now go!" He did as she said without question.

Sasha wasted no time wondering what had just

happened. She had been to GenetiLabs countless times, and she knew exactly where to go: the lab. With crossbow held high and silver nails up, she made her way directly there.

When she arrived at the door, it was wide open, as was the door to the refrigerator. Mason Stout was bringing bags of blood out and packing them into some kind of duffel bag on the lab counter.

"Mason Stout," Sasha said in a quiet voice, "I have come for you."

The man stopped dead in his tracks and spun around in her direction. He took one look at her, his eyes reflecting almost holographically in the moonlight which shone through the window, and he smiled, revealing the whitest, most treacherous teeth she had ever seen.

"I see you have, dear child," he hissed. "Now come to me!"

# CHAPTER 24

Ira Stone saw Sasha run directly up to the guard, and he became very nervous. What was she doing? He watched her speak to the man, and his clear vision showed him the look on the man's face. Ira closed his eyes and spoke to the man with the power of his mind.

"Let her in the building," he whispered, willing the man to submit. "Let her in; she is there to save your life."

He felt it strongly when the guard's will crumbled, and when Ira opened his eyes it was just in time to see the guard unlocking the door for her. He breathed a huge sigh of relief and gave the Dark Father thanks. Sasha would need all the help she could get if Ira were to avoid being revealed.

Once she was inside, Ira climbed from the battered old sedan and walked quickly through the same field she had crossed. He reached GenetiLabs and tried the door Sasha had entered through, but it was locked; it had automatically done so as soon as she'd let it close. His heart sank, but he didn't let it deter him. He rounded the building quickly; he would keep an eye on her through the laboratory windows. There, he crouched down just in time to witness Mason Stone, blood bags in hand, whirling to face the young girl who had just confronted him.

He could barely hear the words the monster spoke. "I see that you have, dear child. Now come to me!"

Ira Stone knew that Stout would not allow the girl to come to him; rather, he would rush her unexpectedly, and Stone was right. Stout placed the blood in his arms on the lab counter, turned back to her, and flew through the air directly at Sasha Hunter. Ira braced himself, and his lips began to seek the Father's strength silently for her.

But Sasha was ready. She swung her left arm with all her might just as he reached her, and the sharp silver blades which tipped her fingers gouged the dead flesh of his face deeply. Mason Stout cried out loudly; it was almost a scream. He lost flight, crashing into a stainless steel cart and hitting the floor with great force.

Sasha reached up and flipped the light switch to the lab, flooding the room with bright fluorescence. Mason Stout's hand was on his cheek, and when he pulled it away, it was coated with black blood. The flesh around the four wounds on his face bubbled and burned as if Sasha had thrown acid on the man.

She stepped back and took a good look at him before beginning to walk around him. His hand went back to his cheek and his eyes, which were so blood-red, as they followed her every move. A chill went down her spine, motivating her to tighten her grip on her crossbow and improve its aim. She wiggled her fingers, brushing the silver tips together, making a painful metallic sound. Mason cringed.

"You bitch!" he suddenly roared. He rose into mid-air and hovered there for a moment before beginning to float, quickly, in her direction. He grabbed at her with his arms, one after the other, rapidly, his long fingernails coming within inches of her face as she stepped back quickly, one step after another.

"Who has led you to me? You are nothing more than a presumptuous child who has no idea who she faces!"

Her back was suddenly against the wall, and Stout lunged at her so fast that he was nothing but a blur. Sasha closed her eyes and quickly withdrew her sword and threw it blindly at him. It took off Mason Stout's left arm.

"Screw you!" she screamed as he flew back ten feet; his arm flying even further. It lay on the floor, flipping and flopping like a fish out of water. Smoke was rising from both the limb on the floor and the stump from which it came.

Mason stared down at the place where his arm used to be, and suddenly looked to the ceiling and screamed. Sasha froze, her eyes wide. All of the demons were encompassed in that scream, and for a fraction of a second, she doubted her ability to win this battle.

After Stout screamed and cried for what seemed like minutes, he staggered to his feet. Was he getting weak? Was the silver doing more than simply slowing down his ability to heal? She found herself praying that she would put an end to this, but it was just the beginning.

Once he was erect, Stout ran from the lab, even leaving his precious cargo of blood behind, and on his way out of the room he turned off the lighting in the lab.

Sasha cried out, startled by his action. Then she remembered: at the last minute she had equipped the crossbow with a tiny Maglite by duct-taping it to the underside. She felt for it and, when she found it, rotated its head. Light poured out before her, and she breathed a sigh of relief.

"Where did you go, you rotten animal?" she screamed. "A little worried, are we? Well, you have nothing to really worry about anymore, because I'm going to tear your soul to pieces!"

Sasha Hunter advanced. She walked out of the lab quickly and turned right down the corridor in the direction she had seen him go. She had one advantage: she knew the place very well. She had visited her father there during his night shift, sometimes for hours. As she walked, she flipped on every light switch she passed.

"I'm coming for you, Mason Stout!"

Her pace was much slower now, as she tried to look into every door she passed. She would stop and reach inside, turning on the lights each time. As she neared the end of the hall, she was aware that she was getting closer to him, and her heart began to pound.

"Here, Mason," she taunted. "Here, Stout. Here, you stinking devil!"

Suddenly, another blur from the right came flying

through the air and hit her forcefully, knocking her against the wall and to the floor. Her head bounced, and in her dizzy state, her only thought was to be thankful that her bow was still gripped tightly in her hand. Right then, something hot and burning dropped on her forehead.

Sasha opened her eyes to see Stout hovering over her. He was smiling, his sharp teeth protruding unnaturally from his mouth. Spit was hanging from his lip, and it had hit her in the head, burning her flesh.

"I'm going to ravage your body," he said, "and then your rotting soul."

Sasha swung her left arm hard and buried all of her silver fingertips into his neck. His head flew back and another unearthly scream shot from his gaping mouth, as smoke rose from the wounds. She yanked once and removed the tips, and she watched, entranced, as the black blood began to flow freely. Mason Stout fell to the side, falling off of her and onto the tiled floor.

His scream sounded like a thousand voices all at once. She could hear both the pain and the anger in it, but she didn't care. Sasha stiffly rose off the floor as quickly as she could and ran to the very end of the hall, where she whirled around to face him. He was still screaming, but it was growing weaker. His red eyes were wide open and glowing bright, and he looked as if he might cry.

Finally, his cries tapered off. Stout met her gaze from where he was lying. He propped himself up on one elbow and gave a sort of soft chuckle, but she could hear the pained whine in his voice. He was no longer smiling.

"You are a troublesome little pest, aren't you?"

He struggled next to right himself and get on his feet, but he was definitely weaker now. He was about fifteen feet from her, but he took three steps back. That was when the smile returned.

Sasha had little time to register it before he charged her. She lifted her crossbow and shot once. The pointed wooden arrow with the silver tip tore through his left shoulder and carried him back a few feet. He landed hard on his bum and slid a bit before stopping. He looked up at her, pain across his face.

Sasha took a single step forward, bow still up. "I'm going to kill you, you know."

Mason grabbed the arrow and pulled it from his shoulder, pain all over his face.

"Not if you can't even hit my heart. You're worthless!"

Then he was in the air again, flying toward her like a rocket ship. She pulled the trigger on her bow, but this time she didn't let up on it. Arrows flew out one at a time, over and over, each one tearing through another part of his body and jerking it around in mid-air as though he were a puppet on a string. But he kept coming, and the arrows were getting low.

When there was only one left, and he was mere feet away, Sasha Hunter improved her aim and pulled the trigger for what she was certain would be the last time. Perhaps being the victor was never meant to be.

The arrow broke free of its home, soared through the air, and zipped through his heart as if it were sent there by the hand of God Himself.

Mason Stout's flight stopped. He hung in the air, dangling, looking down at the end of the slender wooden stake she had just gifted him with. He then looked up at her and met her eyes. Black blood began to pour from his mouth and splash to the floor. Suddenly he fell at her, crashing into her body and sandwiching it between himself and the wall. She clawed at him once with her fingertips catching the gums in his mouth, just as he crashed to the floor, dead at last.

She looked down at her left hand; it had been cut wide open by his tooth.

Her head began to spin, and her vision went black, and Sasha Hunter fell to the floor hard, fainting dead away.

# EPILOGUE

"What are you in the mood for, dear? Steak or chicken?"

Ira Stone and Sasha Hunter sat on the back patio at his luxurious home. Ira was preparing to grill a wonderful meal for the girl he considered to be his daughter. She had been very ill, very ill indeed. As a matter of fact, she had been sleeping for two days. He had gone to the Dark Father and begged that the bite she received bear no grave consequences. He had begged that she enter the Family and be given the gift. He had received no direct answer. When she had awakened, the first thing she had said was, "I'm hungry."

"I think steak sounds wonderful, Ira; thank you."

She offered him a smile then took a sip of the tall glass of iced tea he had brought her. It was early evening, and the sun was setting fast, but the night was warm. Patio lights illuminated the entire area, making it seem homey and inviting.

"What happened, Ira?" she asked suddenly. "I only remember shooting, and then...?"

Ira put the steaks on the hot grill and took his seat at

the patio table. "I was outside, and by the time the noise died down, and I broke the glass to enter Stout was dead, and you were unconscious on the floor. The only harm you seemed to suffer was a tiny cut on your hand. Is it better?"

She looked down at the tiny bandage covering the cut. "I guess. It doesn't hurt if that's what you mean."

"Anyway," he continued, "the authorities arrived and took his body. He was cremated right away. Some wanted to study him, but a court of law fortunately won. Mason Stout is gone for good. Do you feel avenged?"

She smiled shyly and nodded. "I guess so."

"I need to go in the house and grab the seasoning. Do you need anything?" Ira asked.

Sasha shook her head, and Ira disappeared through the sliding glass door. She looked up at the moon in the sky; it was so beautiful and breathtaking. As she gazed at it, she tried to remember her father, but suddenly it seemed she couldn't recall him at all, and she felt a bit confused. Her skin felt prickly and hot, and dizziness seemed to come over her again.

Ira whistled as he stood in the kitchen, grill fork in hand, scanning the cupboard shelf in search of the seasoning. He felt wonderful that Sasha had made it through such a horrifying ordeal. What a strong and determined young lady she was. He was pleased she had come into his life, and he would see to it that she was cared for, for all eternity. If the Father allowed her to join the Family, there was so much he could teach her.

The only thing left to do was tell her the truth: she had suffered a bite, and she was undergoing a change. But he had all the time in the world to do that.

"Got the seasoning," he said as he rejoined her on the patio. She was standing at the edge of it, staring up at the moon as though it were a lover. "Isn't it wonderful?"

"It is," she replied.

He was standing at the grill, sprinkling seasoning on the steak, humming a tune she didn't recognize. Sasha came up behind him and put her arms around him, hugging him from behind.

"Thank you so much for all you have done, Ira."

He turned to her slightly, then back to the meat. "No, Sasha Hunter, thank you. You have no idea what you've done, and for whom you have done it."

"Well," she said lightly, her arms still around his shoulders, "I have a pretty good idea."

With that, she took him by the base of the skull and sliced his head from his body in one deft movement. His body fell to the concrete, where it lay twitching as the blood flowed freely. She flung the head against the brick house and watched, amused, as it hit the ground.

Sasha bent down and took the grill fork from his tightly clenched hand and began to tend her steak. She wanted it very rare, after all. Nice and juicy and full of flavor.

# ENTREATY

This book was made possible by reviews from readers like you. Reviews fuel my creativity. If you enjoyed this novel, I implore you to please write a review and share your experience on the retailer's website. The livelihood for authors is entirely dependent on reviews, and I must say, it is the largest obstacle as a struggling author that I have encountered. Please tell a friend, tell a loved one about this read. With your help, I will be one step closer to overcoming this obstacle. In return, I thank you from the bottom of my heart, and sincerely appreciate your time and effort.

Humbled, with gratitude,

R.W.K. Clark

# ABOUT THE AUTHOR

I am a father of two beautiful children, Jon and Kim. They are my motivating forces; they are the lighthouse in this vast ocean. In my life, they are the air that I breathe; they are the oasis in this desert of uncertainty. They are my greatest joy in life and my number one priority. I have a long list of hobbies, and I attribute that to my lust for life! I like to surround myself with positive people, who share the same interests. Family values, the arts, outdoors, nature, and travel are tops on my list. I embrace attending cultural and artistic events because I believe dramatic self-expression is the window to the soul. I wear my heart on my sleeve, and I still believe in chivalry, and I always treat people the way I want to be treated.

www.rwkclark.com